A Candlelight Ecstasy Romance

"PLEASE, JULIA, DON'T TEMPT ME!"

"Am I?" She felt rather pleased at the prospect.

David groaned softly. "You really don't know what you're doing, do you?"

"Of course I do. I'm trying to get you into bed with me." She looked away from him. So softly that he had to strain to hear her, she murmured, "I was so frightened. Please don't leave me alone."

He stared at her for a long moment, taking in her beauty. His hands clenched at his sides only to relax suddenly as the fight went out of him. "All right, but I want you to promise to respect me in the morning."

CANDLELIGHT ECSTASY ROMANCES®

274 WITH ALL MY HEART, *Emma Bennett*
275 JUST CALL MY NAME, *Dorothy Ann Bernard*
276 THE PERFECT AFFAIR, *Lynn Patrick*
277 ONE IN A MILLION, *Joan Grove*
278 HAPPILY EVER AFTER, *Barbara Andrews*
279 SINNER AND SAINT, *Prudence Martin*
280 RIVER RAPTURE, *Patricia Markham*
281 MATCH MADE IN HEAVEN, *Malissa Carroll*
282 TO REMEMBER LOVE, *Jo Calloway*
283 EVER A SONG, *Karen Whittenburg*
284 CASANOVA'S MASTER, *Anne Silverlock*
285 PASSIONATE ULTIMATUM, *Emma Bennett*
286 A PRIZE CATCH, *Anna Hudson*
287 LOVE NOT THE ENEMY, *Sara Jennings*
288 SUMMER FLING, *Natalie Stone*
289 AMBER PERSUASION, *Linda Vail*
290 BALANCE OF POWER, *Shirley Hart*
291 BEGINNER'S LUCK, *Alexis Hill Jordan*
292 LIVE TOGETHER AS STRANGERS, *Megan Lane*
293 AND ONE MAKES FIVE, *Kit Daley*
294 RAINBOW'S END, *Lori Copeland*
295 LOVE'S DAWNING, *Tate McKenna*
296 SOUTHERN COMFORT, *Carla Neggers*
297 FORGOTTEN DREAMS, *Eleanor Woods*
298 MY KIND OF LOVE, *Barbara Andrews*
299 SHENANDOAH SUMMER, *Samantha Hughes*
300 STAND STILL THE MOMENT, *Margaret Dobson*
301 NOT TOO PERFECT, *Candice Adams*
302 LAUGHTER'S WAY, *Paula Hamilton*
303 TOMORROW'S PROMISE, *Emily Elliott*
304 PULLING THE STRINGS, *Alison Tyler*
305 FIRE AND ICE, *Anna Hudson*
306 ANOTHER SUNNY DAY, *Kathy Clark*
307 OFF LIMITS, *Sheila Paulos*
308 THRILL OF THE CHASE, *Donna Kimel Vitek*
309 DELICATE DIMENSIONS, *Dorothy Ann Bernard*
310 HONEYMOON, *Anna Hudson*
311 LOST LETTERS, *Carol Norris*
312 APPLE OF MY EYE, *Carla Neggers*
313 PRIDE AND JOY, *Cathie Linz*

STAR-CROSSED

Sara Jennings

A CANDLELIGHT ECSTASY ROMANCE®

Published by
Dell Publishing Co., Inc.
1 Dag Hammarskjold Plaza
New York, New York 10017

Copyright © 1985 by Maura Seger

All rights reserved. No part of this book may be reproduced or transmitted in any form or by any means, electronic or mechanical, including photocopying, recording, or by any information storage and retrieval system, without the written permission of the Publisher, except where permitted by law.

Dell ® TM 681510, Dell Publishing Co., Inc.
Candlelight Ecstasy Romance®, 1,203,540, is a registered trademark of Dell Publishing Co., Inc., New York, New York.

ISBN: 0-440-18299-9

Printed in the United States of America
First printing—March 1985

To Our Readers:

We have been delighted with your enthusiastic response to Candlelight Ecstasy Romances®, and we thank you for the interest you have shown in this exciting series.

In the upcoming months we will continue to present the distinctive sensuous love stories you have come to expect only from Ecstasy. We look forward to bringing you many more books from your favorite authors and also the very finest work from new authors of contemporary romantic fiction.

As always, we are striving to present the unique, absorbing love stories that you enjoy most—books that are more than ordinary romance. Your suggestions and comments are always welcome. Please write to us at the address below.

> Sincerely,
>
> The Editors
> Candlelight Romances
> 1 Dag Hammarskjold Plaza
> New York, New York 10017

CHAPTER ONE

"You're sure you want to go all that way by yourself, miss? Desert travel can be tough."

Julia Cabot listened politely to the gas-station attendant. He'd been expressing the same doubts for some twenty minutes, ever since she had turned off the New Mexico highway and pulled up beside the ramshackle building that materialized out of the shimmering heat.

Her tank was only half empty, but the desire for a few minutes of human company and a cold Coke had made up her mind for her. To say that she wasn't used to such desolation was to understate the case.

Coming from the bustle of wintertime Boston, the abrupt change was startling. Perhaps it was just that she was tired, but she found her nerves on edge and the miles she still had to travel hard to contemplate.

Yet she was determined to press on. The job she had come to do was unpleasant enough without dragging it out.

"I'm sure I'll be at my destination before dark," she

said confidently. "But thanks just the same for your concern."

The attendant shrugged skeptically. His weathered features and lean body made it difficult to guess his age. He might have been perched at this way station beside the road forever. "If you say so, miss. This a rental car?"

Julia brushed back a strand of ebony hair that had come loose from the neat chignon at the back of her neck and nodded. "I picked it up at the airport."

"Fine for city driving, but out here things are a little rougher. Four-wheel drive is what you want, with a specially cooled engine and good traction."

"I told the rental agent where I was going."

The man shrugged again. "Probably some city slicker. Don't know beans about what it's like out here. The desert can be real deceptive." Gesturing toward the vast expanse of emptiness surrounding them, he added, "Looks right peaceful out there, don't it?"

As a matter of fact, it didn't. Julia had been in lonely places before, most recently within her own spirit. But not even they had prepared her for the sheer scope of the sea of sand that seemed to mock the tiny humans who dared to challenge it.

She must be tired, she thought wearily, closing her violet eyes for a moment. There was a deep core of sadness inside her that lay like a cold stone. Lately it seemed to be swelling, as though threatening to overtake her entirely.

Impatient with herself, Julia straightened abruptly. She had everything in the world to be happy about: good health, fairly good looks, plenty of money, and a thriving business. Up until recently that had all seemed more than enough. Until some change occurred within her and what began as a pebble of discontent grew into a cold stone.

She was paying too much attention to herself; better to concentrate on someone else. As the attendant cleaned her dusty windshield, she asked, "Have you lived here long?"

The man snorted good-naturedly. "All my life. My pa was a miner, had a little shack back there aways."

Again, Julia studied the barren land that bore no signs of life except for patches of chaparral and cactus. Heat turned the sky to a blurred haze and drifted up from the sand in a shimmering mist. There was no clear dividing line between earth and sky. They seemed to merge into each other with almost dizzying effect.

There was an otherworldly quality to the land that contrasted sharply with her memory of lush green forests and foam-crested oceans. No wonder men came to such a place to dream of leaving the earth. There was little here to make them want to stay.

"Did you ever think about going somewhere else?" she asked gently.

The attendant stuck the rag back in his pocket and regarded her solemnly. "Nope, can't say I did. Got everything I want right here. I've seen plenty of people come up and down this road, but not many of 'em seemed happier than me."

His obvious sincerity impressed Julia. She wondered what it felt like to feel so certain of anything.

Her own life had been in upheaval since the death of her uncle six months before. At twenty-five, she had found herself heir by default to his responsibilities as head of the family's venture capital firm. Very simply, no one else wanted the job.

"You're the logical choice, Julia," her mother had said when they met for tea in her flower-filled sitting room overlooking the garden of the elegant house Grandfather Cabot had built sixty years before. Beyond the lace-curtained windows was the green swathe of Boston Commons, dotted with children at play and couples strolling together.

A sigh had escaped Julia as she smoothed the neatly tailored skirt of the black suit she had worn to the funeral. "I don't think I'm really the best person for the job, Mother. After all, it isn't as though I've had much business training."

"You can hire people who have that, dear. The point is the firm must be run by someone in the family." A slight smile had touched her mother's lovely, well-preserved face.

"What about Stewart?" Julia had asked even as she suspected she knew the answer. Her elder brother was "finding himself" in the mountains of northern Colorado. The chance of him giving a moment's attention to anything as mundane as earning a living was remote.

Her mother had wrinkled her nose delicately. "Let's not get into that, dear. The fact is it's up to you to protect our interests. You're certainly bright enough. Look how well you did at Bryn Mawr."

"That was different, Mother. I was an art history major."

"A perfectly suitable interest for you at the time. But things have changed."

They must have, she had thought wryly, to force her mother to turn to her. They had never been close: Belinda Cabot preferred to devote her attentions to her husband and son. She was a man's woman, uninterested in those of her own sex, including her daughter.

But with Stewart Cabot, Senior, dead and Junior at what his mother charitably described as an "awkward" stage, she had no choice. The family fortune, and her own very comfortable life-style, stood in jeopardy. Julia would, of course, do her duty.

She did, but not without hesitation and doubts her mother could not possibly have understood. Plunged unprepared into the world of high finance, she had had to draw on all her resources to survive.

Her initial feelings of apprehension were soon followed by eighteen-hour days and, more often than not, sleepless nights. In six months she had changed from a quiet, somewhat shy girl to a fiercely determined woman.

Pride had come to her rescue; the fierce Cabot pride that would not tolerate failure. By any objective measure, she was a somewhat surprising but nonetheless indisputable success. Only on occasion, as now, did she wonder if it was all really worth the price she was paying.

It might be nice to just sit and watch the world go by for a while. She could barely remember what relaxation meant. Sometimes in the privacy of her bedroom, in the narrow twin bed she had never shared, she wanted to cry out against the injustice of it all. The pressure was often almost intolerable, yet she was always expected to carry on as though there was no problem she could not solve.

Like now. Her generous mouth tightened as she thought about why she had come to New Mexico. Skyward, Inc., was the only one of her uncle's investments she thought was a dud.

It was beyond her how staid, sensible Uncle Thaddeus had ever decided to invest in a private venture to launch satellites into space. Perhaps it was true that everyone had a secret romantic streak, but in Uncle Thad's case, it had been deeply buried.

David Sherwood, the renegade astronaut who was the guiding light behind Skyward, must have done an incredible job of salesmanship to wring so much money out of an intensely conservative Boston Brahmin.

Which was one more good reason to be suspicious of the man she was going to meet. Finishing her

Coke, Julia mentally reviewed the information provided by the investigative firm she had put to work on the case.

David Sherwood was thirty-three years old with a master's degree in astrophysics from M.I.T. and a reputation as an inveterate tinkerer in high technology. He had married young, straight out of high school, and promptly ended up in Vietnam, where he spent two years as a prisoner of war.

While he was gone, his wife divorced him and both his parents died. He came home to a world in which he seemed to have no place, yet had still managed to carve out a career for himself almost any other man would envy.

After several jobs with various companies—all with increasingly high levels of responsibility and salary—he had gone to work for NASA. Rising quickly through the astronaut ranks, he had piloted several missions of the space shuttle before abruptly resigning.

The reason for his departure was not clear, but it seemed Sherwood had rebelled against the impersonality of the government-run agency. He claimed that it was time for private enterprise to become involved in space exploration.

Julia grimaced as she thought about that. She knew no more about the space program than any relatively well-informed citizen, but she couldn't imagine a small, privately owned company competing with

NASA, which had the resources of the United States Government and military behind it.

Yet Sherwood clearly believed he could do just that. At least, he had convinced Uncle Thaddeus that he could. Cabot Venture Financing had sunk several million dollars into Skyward.

Julia had no real hope of getting it back, but she was leaning toward cutting her firm's losses and severing her connection with David Sherwood and his harebrained scheme. The purpose of this trip was to make her final decision.

"That'll be twelve dollars, miss, with the Coke."

The voice of the attendant drew Julia out of her thoughts. She fumbled with her purse, finding the catch of the calfskin bag stiff and unwieldy. When she was at last able to fish out her wallet and hand him the bills, the man looked at her with concern.

"You be careful now, miss. There's nothing between here and Arroyo 'cept empty road and emptier desert." He looked at her quizzically. "Say, is that where you're headed, Arroyo?"

"Yes," Julia admitted warily. She couldn't help but anticipate what this weathered old geezer would say about David Sherwood and his crew. But the attendant surprised her. He whistled softly and grinned at her.

"Those space folks sure are something else, aren't they? I remember watching launches back in the sixties. Always thought it was kind of interesting but couldn't quite see what the fuss was about, not even with those moon landings. Wasn't nothing really 'cept another big government boondoggle. But this is different."

Julia paused with her hand on the ignition. "Why do you say that?"

"Why because this is real people, of course, doing real stuff. I been out there to watch them. They run around in chinos and sweat like the rest of us. Ain't much difference that I can see, 'cept they've got a dream. A big one."

He rubbed a hand over his whiskered jaw thoughtfully. "Just imagine what it'll mean if they make it. Instead of space being for sky jockeys and bureaucrats, it'll be for regular folks. Kind of like the people who must have gone along with that Viking who came here, and Columbus. I'll tell you, I'll be plumb glad to have lived to see that day."

As though taken aback by his own unaccustomed verbosity, the attendant flushed. " 'Scuse me for rattling on like that, miss. But when you get to Arroyo, you'll see what I mean."

Julia doubted that, but she was not so insensitive as to tell the man that she had come not to appreciate David Sherwood's great dream but quite probably to close it down. Instead she merely nodded and made her farewells. Moments later she was back on the empty road heading southeast toward Arroyo.

According to her map, she had another hundred miles or so to travel to her destination. With no other vehicles in sight, she felt free to let the powerful car stretch a bit. The speedometer was at seventy before she decided that was too risky on a road she had never driven on before and slowed down.

As she did so, she heard a faint "ping" from somewhere under the hood. For an instant, she stiffened. But when she didn't hear the noise again and the car continued to ride smoothly, she dismissed it.

Julia had gone about another thirty miles when she realized that the air-conditioning system was beginning to fail. With an irate sigh, she snapped it off and pulled over to the side of the road to roll down the windows. As she started up again, she thought the car hesitated slightly, but she couldn't be sure.

Even with the brisk breeze engendered by her speed, the heat was inescapable. Her sensible beige linen dress no longer seemed cool enough. Strands of hair clung to the back of her neck. Her head pounded and the dryness of her throat and mouth became painful. The Coke she had drunk such a short time before seemed like a mirage.

The car sputtered again, followed by an ominous grinding sound. Julia stiffened and slowed down. That precaution proved ineffective as steam began to escape from under the hood.

With a muffled exclamation, she pulled over to the side of the road and hastily turned off the ignition. Getting out, she gingerly put a hand on the hood, only to yank it back quickly and barely escape being burned.

When she touched it again it was with a handkerchief wound around her hand. Working swiftly, she managed to unfasten the catch and threw up the hood. Great clouds of steam engulfed her, causing her to back away hurriedly.

Only when the vapor had cleared enough for her to see did she lean forward again, frowning in bewilderment. She knew next to nothing about cars. They had always been left to the family chauffeur. Peering suspiciously at the jumble of strange mechanical objects, she futilely tried to determine what the problem might be.

Whatever the problem was, she was sure that the heat was to blame. Even as she entertained nasty thoughts about the car rental agency, she was thinking about how to get help.

The gas station was a good eighty miles behind her. By car, she was only minutes from Arroyo, but that wouldn't do her any good now. No one at Skyward knew she was on her way there. She had deliberately kept her visit a surprise.

At the other end, none of her well-trained staff back in Boston expected to hear from her any time soon. They were accustomed to being left on their own when she was away on business trips.

Nor would her mother be more than mildly annoyed when she failed to call. Belinda was in the midst of planning for the annual Garden Club gala. It would be days, if not longer, before she began to wonder where her daughter had gone.

Julia tilted her head back and stared at the sky

warily. A cluster of birds circled lazily off in the distance. She shivered slightly, not wanting to think about what they might be, and looked away.

A glance at her luggage brought home to her her inadequate preparations for the desert. Expecting to be at Skyward's headquarters no more than a day, she had brought her handbag, briefcase, and a change of underclothes. Hardly appropriate for the present situation.

In the back of her mind she remembered hearing that people stranded in the desert should remain with their vehicles because eventually they would be found.

The sticking point was that *eventually*. She was not given to waiting around, especially when her life might be at stake. How long could it take to walk twenty miles? A few hours, at most.

She was certainly in good enough shape for such a trek. Never mind that she didn't look particularly athletic. Not everyone could be tall and willowy. Some had to be content with medium height and unfashionable curves. But that was no reason to believe she didn't have plenty of stamina. Besides, what choice did she have?

She found intolerable the idea of help being so close at hand yet out of reach. With the swift decisiveness she had been forced to adopt in recent months, she grabbed her handbag and briefcase, locked the car, and started off.

She walked for perhaps half an hour before she

began to fully feel the heat. Not a breath of air stirred around her. The sun beat down mercilessly, baking her head. Her ivory skin began to feel uncomfortably tight and strained, and the pain in her head developed into an almost blinding ache.

Her nylon panty hose became intolerable, as did her seemingly practical shoes. She tottered on the heels, feeling the searing throb of the asphalt through the thin soles.

For a moment a hint of fear flickered in her thick-fringed eyes. She suppressed it instantly. She'd been in tougher spots; seated across the table from some of the wiliest, most unscrupulous deal-makers in the business, forced to best them to protect her family's interests. More often than not she came out with what she wanted.

Being stranded in the desert wasn't precisely the same thing, but she was still confident of her ability to successfully extricate herself from a ticklish situation. In no time at all she'd be sitting somewhere nice and cool, sipping a gin and tonic and laughing at the whole mess.

Another half an hour passed and Julia's expectations wilted. She decided she'd settle for shade and anything drinkable. Twenty miles were proving to be far longer than she had figured. What seemed perfectly possible in theory was turning out to be impossible in actuality.

Perhaps another car would come along. Her head hurt too much to twist it around, but she could look straight ahead for miles and see that there was nothing in sight. Those darned birds were in front of her now and there seemed to be a gnat buzzing at her ear.

She tried to brush it away but the sound continued, growing into a steady drone. Her briefcase and purse seemed very heavy. She wished she had left them in the car. But then she would have arrived at Skyward without the badge of her authority.

That thought made her giggle. She wasn't going to look any too impressive when she finally did get there. Not unless David Sherwood had a thing for particularly wilted ladies with straggly hair, sunburned skin, and dazed expressions.

The soles of her feet began to hurt so much that she could no longer ignore them. Nylon rubbing against the heat-seared skin was torturous. She paused and pondered what to do.

Logically, she should take off her panty hose. But how could she do that in the middle of an open road? Precepts of decorum and modesty drummed into her since childhood made that impossible.

Another giggle escaped her. Imagine worrying about such a thing. If anyone saw her, she would be delighted because it would mean rescue was near.

Slipping her hands under her skirt, she rolled down the offending garment and eased out of it. For a brief moment she felt some relief as the air touched her bare skin. But the sensation faded quickly when she put her shoes back on and started off again.

If only she had something to put on her head. Back home in the closet of her bedroom was a wide-brimmed straw hat she had worn on picnics when she was still able to indulge in such pastimes. What she would give to have it with her now.

And while she was at it, how about a well-chilled glass of champagne and a bowl of strawberries dusted with powdered sugar? That would go down marvelously.

The tip of her tongue touched her dry lips and she frowned. When had they become so cracked? She hadn't been walking that long, had she? Maybe she should just sit down for a few minutes. At least long enough to catch her breath.

She hadn't been walking fast, just plodding along, one step after another. Yet her heart was racing as though she had just run a mile and she couldn't seem to draw in enough air.

Panting, she slumped against a rock. She'd just close her eyes long enough to ease the aching glare. There was that gnat again, still buzzing, louder than ever. And the birds, she could see them even with her eyes shut. Great black things whirling in the heat-hazed sky.

There was a rush of wings, or was it panic fluttering within her? Not that it mattered. The sensation passed so swiftly it might never have been.

She was too exhausted to be afraid. Her cracked lips moved in a faint smile. It was years since she'd slept during the day, but just this once she'd make an exception.

She nodded to herself at the wisdom of her decision. Sleep during the heat of the day and travel at night. That was the sensible thing to do. If only she had some shade . . . and some water. Better not to think about that. She was so thirsty.

Her eyes flickered, opened for a moment, then closed again. She shook her head dazedly. The desert before her seemed to be turning into a great shimmering pool of water.

With her last ounce of energy she bent toward it, not feeling the harsh grains of sand against her skin. The water was so lovely . . . cool and soft. Just in time. It would wash away all the dirt and heat and give her the strength to go on.

Soon she would have nothing more to worry about.

CHAPTER TWO

"She's a lucky one," a low voice murmured. "A few more hours out there and she would have been buzzard bait."

"Maybe that's what should have happened," a second voice said. "Anyone dumb enough to do what she did doesn't deserve to survive."

"Ah, come on now, you don't really mean that."

"Don't I? We tell people over and over not to wander around in the desert and do they listen? No way. Instead they get themselves into all sorts of trouble and people like me end up having to rescue them."

Julia frowned. The voice sounded so angry. She wanted to get away from it, but when she tried to move she found her body would not respond. It was all she could do to mutter faintly.

"What was that?" the first voice demanded, startled.

"I think she said something," the second muttered dryly. "Some slur on my chivalry, it sounded like."

Julia's eyes flickered open. She had to get a look at the owner of that wryly sarcastic tone. Who did he think he was anyway, acting as though what had happened was her fault? Never mind that maybe it was. He should be polite enough not to say so. A rim of bright light struck her eyes, making her flinch.

"Turn the lamp down," the gentler voice instructed. "Her eyes can't take it."

Soothing dimness touched her. She ventured another look and found herself in a small, simply furnished room. Aside from the bed she was lying in, there was only a wooden worktable that looked as though it doubled as a desk and a couple of straight-back chairs occupied by the two men.

One was in his fifties, with a kindly face and reassuring manner. When he spoke she wasn't surprised to discover his was the gentler voice. "How are you feeling, little lady?"

"A-all right . . ."

The other man snorted disparagingly, drawing her attention to him. Even seated, it was obvious that he was tall and possessed the wiry leanness of a long-distance runner. Yet his shoulders and chest were broad, suggesting strength as well as stamina.

His angular face was tanned in startling contrast to his sun-washed blond hair and light blue eyes. As Julia's gaze met his, she was swept by contradictory emotions.

On the one hand, she was annoyed by what he had said about her and by the scathing derision of his look. On the other, she was appalled to discover that some perverse trick of fate had made him attractive to her on a most elemental level.

A quiver of mingled apprehension and anticipation shimmered through her as she told herself her reaction was nothing more than the lingering effects of too much sun. She swallowed painfully and felt for the first time how parched and swollen her throat had become. "H-how long . . ."

"How long were you out there?" Blue Eyes finished for her. His beautifully etched mouth twisted sardonically. "A couple of hours, I'd guess. You were completely out of your head when I found you." He laughed disdainfully. "Or maybe that's just your normal state."

Julia found his sarcasm hard to take. Still terribly weak and well aware of how close she had come to tragedy, she had few defenses left. To her humiliation, she found herself close to tears and turned her face away in a futile effort to hide them.

Blue Eyes muttered something impatiently. An unexpectedly gentle hand touched a cool, smooth handkerchief to her cheeks. "Don't start in on that," he advised gruffly. "It won't make you feel any better."

"What do you expect her to do?" the older man intervened. "Poor little thing was probably scared out of her wits."

Julia opened her mouth to assure them she had been anything but, then thought better of it. She hardly needed to flaunt her poor judgment more than she had already done.

"I'll be going now," her defender went on. "Just keep her in bed, get plenty of liquids into her, and use the cream I'm leaving."

"Thanks, Doc," Blue Eyes said. "I appreciate your coming out here so fast."

"Won't be the last time somebody gets hauled in out of the desert. Keep in mind she's obviously a city girl and don't be too rough on her. And as for you, miss"—Julia opened her eyes a sliver—"don't plan on doing any sunbathing any time soon. You were lucky to pass out facedown with your legs tucked under you. That saved you from second-degree burns, at the least. But you're still going to be feeling stiff and sore for a few days."

He patted her hand reassuringly, picked up his bag, and headed for the door. Blue Eyes went with him. Julia heard them talking just outside the room but couldn't make out what they were saying. She fought to stay awake but fell inexorably back into sleep.

When she woke again it was dark in the room. Night had fallen and the curtains were drawn across the only window. The weather was surprisingly cool, so much so that she was grateful for the thin blanket covering her.

Her throat felt better. She had a dim recollection of someone lifting her several times and urging her to drink. A carafe of ice water and a glass stood on a table beside the bed. Suddenly aware of her continued thirst, she sat up quickly to pour herself some water. The covers fell away, revealing that she was naked.

A soft exclamation escaped her. Who had undressed her? The doctor, hopefully, or . . . ? For reasons she couldn't explain, the thought of Blue Eyes removing her clothes was not as distasteful as it should have been. Firmly pushing that possibility aside, she reached for the water.

As she did so, the door opened and the object of her speculation strolled in. Julia set the glass down hastily and grabbed for the covers, pulling them back over her as she glared at him. "Don't you believe in knocking?"

He looked startled, then grinned as his eyes settled on her hands tightly clutching the sheet and blanket over her breasts. Not at all repentantly, he murmured, "Sorry, I didn't think you'd be awake. Not that it matters. I saw all there was to see when I brought you in."

Julia's mouth tightened in a hard line that belied the soft fluttering in her stomach. "It figures that you'd have to tell me that. Why didn't you wait for the doctor?"

Strolling over to the bed, he sat down beside her and filled the glass, handing it to her before he answered. "Because I had no idea how badly off you might be. What you did to yourself was idiotic; peo-

27

ple have died from such stunts. You were damn lucky I found you."

Julia took a sip of the cool water reluctantly, not wanting to accept anything from such an odious man but unable to deny her thirst. Stiffly, she said, "I do appreciate your rescuing me."

"Thanks," the man said dryly. "When you're feeling stronger I'll let you overwhelm me with gratitude. In the meantime, you're going to stay here and do exactly as Doc ordered."

"Just where is 'here'?"

"Arroyo." As though belatedly remembering his manners, her host said, "I'm David Sherwood."

Julia sighed resignedly. She wasn't surprised to learn where she was; with so few settlements in the area, it was natural that someone from Arroyo had found her. But did it really have to be Sherwood? Looking up, she met his eyes reluctantly. "I'm Julia Cabot, Mr. Sherwood. I was on my way here to see you about . . ."

"I know who you are," he interjected, "and it isn't hard to figure out the reason for your impromptu visit. Fact is, ever since Thaddeus died, I've been expecting you."

Julia raised an eyebrow, nonplussed as much by his awareness of her identity as by his apparent familiarity with her uncle. Very few people had referred to the late head of Cabot Venture Finance by his first name.

"You must have known my uncle well," she began

in a tone that made it clear she believed anything but.

David grinned sardonically. "You'd be surprised. There were sides of Thaddeus I'd be willing to bet he kept pretty well hidden." His expression became slightly more gentle as he added, "I'll miss him. He was a friend as well as a partner."

Julia edged down beneath the covers. She didn't know what to say to him. Uncle Thaddeus had been an important and dearly loved part of her life. He had often stood as a buffer between her and her uncaring parents, doing everything he could to make her feel cherished and secure.

But she had always had the impression that few other people appreciated his generally taciturn, demanding personality. Now here was this stranger who had apparently been on excellent terms with him.

Maybe it was better to just change the subject. "You said you know why I'm here?"

His expression hardened. "It's not hard to guess. You want to close down Skyward."

The sheer bluntness of that took her breath away. She was used to even the most ruthless conduct being dressed up in pretty euphemisms. "I'm giving consideration to withdrawing my firm's financial support," she said carefully. "You'll be perfectly free to find backing elsewhere."

"People who believe in free enterprise space flight

29

and have money to invest aren't exactly falling out of the trees," he replied coldly.

Tempted though she was to point out that, in her considered opinion, there were also very few people who believed in Santa Claus or the Tooth Fairy, Julia restrained herself. The last thing she wanted to do was to get into an argument with a man she barely knew while lying stark naked in bed.

"Look," she managed with far more firmness than she felt, "let's just postpone this discussion until I'm up and about, all right? I promise I won't inconvenience you by staying a moment longer than necessary."

"You're already inconveniencing me," David informed her flatly. His sky-blue eyes darkened slightly as he added, "This happens to be my bed you're occupying."

"Why didn't you put me somewhere else?" Julia demanded. She had the horrifying thought that he knew exactly what sort of response his words had evoked and was thoroughly enjoying her discomfiture.

"Where would you suggest? There's the bunkhouse for the mechanics plus a few cottages for the scientists and me. That's the sum total of our palatial accommodations." His mouth tightened as he added, "We're not exactly running a resort hotel here, you know. This is serious business."

"I can do perfectly well with a sleeping bag and a

quiet corner somewhere," she informed him tartly, flushing at his sardonic laugh.

"Sure you could. You're a regular outdoorsman . . . uh . . . person. Let's indulge in a little honesty here, Ms. Cabot. You don't know your Boston beans about taking care of yourself in the desert. You proved that more than adequately when you walked away from your car."

A wave of anger rolled toward her as he thought back to how she had been when he found her. "Don't you realize what you could have done to yourself? Dehydration and sunstroke can kill within a matter of hours. And if you do manage to survive, it's not unheard of to suffer permanent damage to internal organs, including the brain."

"There's nothing wrong with my brain, Mr. Sherwood, or any other part of me," she shot back, determined to hide the shiver of fear his words provoked. "I appreciate your care, but I don't see any reason why I have to listen to a tirade. You obviously deeply resent my presence here and you've seized on this unfortunate incident to embarrass and undermine me."

It was a vintage performance by the "new" Julia Cabot, businesswoman *extraordinaire*. More than one chauvinistic business competitor had had his confidence shriveled by her cool disdain. But it didn't faze David in the least. He merely shrugged and looked down at her with an expression suspiciously similar to amused tolerance.

"Look, maybe I am being too hard on you. You've been through a hell of an experience and Doc would have my head if he knew I was upsetting you. So let's just forget it, for the moment. Get some sleep, and if you need anything during the night, I'll be in the next room."

As he stood up to leave, Julia stared after him. She was working hard at being angry at him when she shouldn't have had to work at it at all. He was sarcastic, disparaging, and threatening in a way she didn't even want to recognize. Yet he made her feel things she had never experienced before.

Lying in his bed, stripped of the clothes he had removed, she felt startlingly vulnerable yet comfortable. Grudgingly, she told herself there were worse places to recover from sunstroke. By tomorrow she would be her old self again and then David Sherwood would learn a thing or two!

Having decided that, she should have been able to sleep, but rest eluded her. When she closed her eyes, she could see the vivid images of the desert filling her first with apprehension and then with mounting fear.

She was so small and alone in the immense sea of sand. Her life was little more than a flickering candle flame cast against the sun. It would be swallowed up in an instant.

Terror grew in her as the full extent of her own helplessness weighed heavily. She cried out, writhing on the bed in a futile effort to escape, only to be startled into stillness when David's face and form drifted before her. His voice echoed in her ears; the crisp, clean scent of his skin filled her breath; she even imagined she could feel the touch of his hands on her fevered body.

"Julia . . . take it easy . . . you'll be all right."

She sobbed softly, drawn irresistibly to the phantom voice and hands, yet afraid they would vanish. She had to get back to the car, to the gas station and the kindly attendant, to the airport and Boston. She had no place in this alien world of wind-carved buttes and star-seeking men.

"Sit up a little . . . that's right. Don't be afraid. You'll feel better soon." A blessedly cool, damp cloth touched her skin, flowing over her arms and throat, hesitating over the swell of her breasts, moving on finally to the flat plane of her belly and down over her slender legs before beginning again.

She was so hot . . . Nanny had turned the radiator up too high. She'd get out of bed and turn it down, except that she was frightened by the dark shadows in the room high up under the eaves of the Beacon Hill house.

What was she thinking of? She wasn't a little girl anymore. She was twenty, home from college, summering at the Cape on the wide stretch of beach where she loved to lie and dream away the hours. The sun must be too bright. Better be careful or she would get burned.

Burned . . . Uncle Thaddeus had insisted on being cremated. He'd written that into his will, to the shock of his family. Generations of Cabots were buried in the Old North Church cemetery, but not him. His ashes were scattered over the sea, under a starlit sky, just as he had requested in the private letter left for Julia.

She'd gone alone to do that, except for the helicopter pilot, weeping quietly, missing Uncle Thad and wishing he was with her. She felt so alone . . . so bewildered. There was so much to do, all of it hard, like shutting down Skyward.

David's face swam before her. He looked tense and grim, probably angry at her again. She tried to push him away, but he restrained her gently. "You're feverish, Julia. I have to get your temperature down."

Her eyes opened and she stared at him bemusedly. He was naked to the waist, his broad chest gleaming in the dim light of the bedside lamp. Soft golden hair formed a downy mat on either side of his breastbone, tapering into a narrow line across his flat abdomen. So different from herself . . . With artless curiosity she reached to touch him.

David started but made no effort to remove her hand. "Julia," he asked gently, "do you know what you're doing?"

She smiled innocently. "You're furry . . . like my teddy bear."

He tried to choke back a groan only to have it get mixed up with a laugh. "Great, just what I needed. You're gorgeous, naked, sexy as hell, and what do I remind you of . . . ?"

"I always slept with my teddy bear," Julia informed him ingenuously, lost again in memories. "In fact . . ." She hesitated a moment, debating the wisdom of sharing such a confidence, then decided she could trust him. ". . . I still have Teddy. He's on my dresser at home." A giggle escaped her. "But don't tell anyone that, all right? I have to be grown up now."

David shook his head ruefully. "I only wish you were. Honey, you're the sweetest combination of innocence and sensuality I've ever come across and the only reason I'm telling you that is because I know you're out of your head and won't remember a thing. Which is just as well since you're driving me stark-raving nuts."

Julia gazed up at him limpidly. She felt cool now and very relaxed, thanks to him. "I don't want to do that. You're nice to me."

"Like Teddy?" he inquired sardonically.

"Not exactly . . . you're . . . different . . ."

"I'm so glad you noticed. I suggest you remember that."

"Don't go . . . I don't want to be alone."

"Julia . . ."

"Didn't you tell me . . . ? I remember, this is your bedroom. Right?"

"Yes, but you're using it now."

"Doesn't matter," she insisted as she scooted over in the bed and smiled at him. "See, it's big enough for two."

35

David stood over her, his hands on his lean hips. He wore only low-slung blue pajama bottoms she thought went very nicely with his eyes. "You're dressed for bed."

"And you're not dressed at all."

"Oh . . ." She thought about that for a moment but couldn't get too worked up over it. Perhaps he had something against nudity. "Don't you like me this way?"

"Yes," he said very patiently. "That's the problem."

She frowned, trying to understand. "I don't get it . . ."

His mouth quirked up at the corners. "Keep going this way and you just might."

"If this is your room, where are you sleeping?"

"On the couch."

"Aren't you uncomfortable?"

"I'm getting there."

"If you join me, you'll feel better."

"Please, Julia, don't tempt me!"

"Am I?" She felt rather pleased at the prospect.

David groaned softly. "You really don't know what you're doing, do you?"

"Of course I do. I'm trying to get you into bed with me." She looked away from him. So softly that he had to strain to hear her, she murmured, "I . . . was so frightened out there. Please don't leave me alone."

He stared at her for a long moment, taking in the silken fall of ebony hair drifting over her shoulders,

36

the innate fragility of her body that nonetheless seemed to house such strength, and the wide, almost childlike quality of her violet gaze when she reluctantly met his eyes. His hands clenched at his sides, only to relax suddenly as the fight went out of him.

"All right, but I want you to promise to still respect me in the morning."

That struck her as somehow funny. She giggled as he joined her under the covers. In the narrow bed, it was impossible to keep any distance between them. His greater weight depressed the mattress so that she rolled toward him.

The touch of his hard body against hers was infinitely reassuring. Julia sighed contentedly and snuggled closer. "This is very nice. Better than my teddy."

"I can't tell you what that means to me."

"Hmmm . . . I'm so sleepy."

His chest rose and fell in a long sigh. Her head rested on his broad shoulder, her slender legs entwined with his. He raised his arms hesitantly, then gently brought them down around her. "Rest, Julia," he murmured. "You're safe now."

CHAPTER THREE

Julia frowned in her sleep. She was having the strangest dream. Something about a giant teddy bear . . . She stirred slightly, nestling closer to the large, warm body beside her.

Body? Her eyes jerked open. She sat up hastily, her mouth opening in a soundless exclamation of shock as she viewed the man beside her.

David Sherwood? She had gone to bed with David Sherwood? How could she? She barely knew the man, besides which she simply didn't, ever, behave like that.

Tugging the sheet higher over her breasts, she wiggled as far away as she could get without taking her eyes from him. That was a mistake.

The covering slipped from his chest, revealing the broad, sun-bronzed expanse that had so enthralled her the night before. Before she realized what she was doing, she had bared the taut plane of his abdomen clear to his hips and the low-riding band of the blue pajama bottoms.

She dropped the sheet as though burned, but could not avert her gaze. Even asleep and unaware, he was magnificent. She had never before had the opportunity to study a man under such circumstances.

Something deep and strong stirred within her. She tried to still it, but failed. Her breath quickened, and any thoughts she had had about escaping before he awoke evaporated into the warm desert air.

David moved in his sleep and murmured something indiscernible. Julia watched his lips with fascination. She wondered what they would feel like against her own. Had she found out last night, only to forget?

That possibility was frustrating, not to mention embarrassing. He didn't strike her as the sort of man who would take advantage of a woman under any circumstances. Yet how else to explain his presence in her bed?

Her forehead wrinkled as she remembered something about asking him to stay with her. The fiery blush that spread over her cheeks rivaled her sunburn. As her mind cleared, memories from the previous night returned to her.

She remembered her near-tragic mistake in deciding to leave the car and strike out on her own, the overwhelming heat, and her own exhaustion. There had been a doctor, soothing words contrasted with angry ones, unexpected tenderness and care. . . .

She inhaled sharply as she remembered the gentleness with which he had looked after her during the night. The man she had read about in the investigative reports did not seem the sort who would trouble himself in such a way. He could easily have called the doctor back or turned her over to someone else. Even as part of her wished he had done either just so she wouldn't feel indebted to him, she could not restrain a spurt of pleasure.

That treacherous sensation prompted a twinge of dismay. She reined herself in sharply. It wouldn't do to forget the purpose of her visit or the fact that she and David Sherwood were destined to be, at best, ships that passed in the night.

Not for nothing had she been born and bred in Boston. Drawing the sheet with her, she stifled her baser impulses and rose from the bed. Determinedly turning her back on him, she began searching for her clothes.

Her handbag and briefcase were on the table across the room. On a chair beside it her dress and lingerie were neatly folded. Her shoes were on the floor.

As she reached an unsteady hand for the garments, she was drawn up short by a sudden growl from the bed. "Just what do you think you're doing?"

Clutching the sheet with one hand and her dress with the other, Julia turned to face him. She drew herself up to her full five feet, four inches, looked him straight in the eye because that seemed the safest place, and said, "I'm getting dressed, obviously."

"Not in that stuff you aren't." Leaving the bed as

unself-consciously as though they had woken up together every morning of their lives, he strode toward her. His big hand reached for the dress even as his eyes wandered over her leisurely. They held a light of knowledge and appreciation that made it difficult for her to breathe.

"As long as you're here, you'll dress properly."

As much as she loathed an undignified struggle, Julia refused to let go of the dress. She wasn't about to be bullied by him. "There's nothing wrong with this. Besides, I didn't bring anything else."

"So I noticed. Do you always travel so light or were you just confident you wouldn't be here very long?"

When she didn't answer, but contented herself with a glare, he laughed softly. His gaze was somewhat bemused as he murmured, "I thought you'd be taller."

Curious despite herself, Julia raised an eyebrow. "Why?"

"The way Thad described you, I suppose. It was always 'Julia this . . .' and 'Julia that. . . .' He had enormous affection as well as respect for you."

She looked away hastily, unwilling to let him see how his mention of her uncle had affected her. If he had set out to shake her, he was succeeding. "I'd like to get dressed now if you don't mind . . ."

"Oh, but I do. You'll wait until I can find you something sensible to wear."

"I am not accustomed to standing around in a sheet, Mr. Sherwood," she informed him coolly.

He grinned down at her. "Why not? You look very fetching. Of course, you look even more fetching without anything on at all . . ."

"Never mind about that!" Julia snapped. "Would you kindly leave me alone?"

"All right," David agreed with suspicious amicability. As she was trying to ferret out his intentions, he took advantage of her preoccupation to wrest the dress from her hands. Ignoring her affronted yelp, he strolled out of the room, pausing only long enough to glance back at her over his shoulder. "Very fetching," he repeated teasingly, "even if you are a little short."

"I am not short . . ." Julia protested futilely as the door closed behind him. In a highly uncharacteristic fit of pique, she threw the remainder of her clothes after him.

The tiny bundle of silk and lace did not make an impressive weapon. It scattered on the floor even as she whirled around and headed for the bathroom, hoping a cool shower would take the sting out of her temper as well as her sunburn.

By the time she reemerged, the bed had been made and a fresh pile of clothes lay on the worktable. Julia approached them gingerly. She shook her head in astonishment as she surveyed what her unwilling host apparently expected her to wear.

A giggle rose in her throat as she held up the clean but bedraggled pair of cut-offs and the worn chambray shirt. Both were as far from her business wardrobe as could be imagined. How surprised he would be to learn that she had spent the happiest times of her life in similar clothes.

The summers she'd spent on the Cape were a precious memory. Those halcyon days of contentment and confidence were far removed from her present demanding existence. What harm could there be in recapturing some small part of them, especially since that meant dressing in what was admittedly a far more practical fashion for her surroundings.

Beneath the clothes she found a tube of suntan cream and a note written in an unmistakably authoritative hand: "Use this." Much as she disliked his tendency to order her around, she was too sensible to reject what was obviously essential to her comfort and well-being. Yesterday only the peculiar angle of her fall when she slipped into unconsciousness had saved her from being badly burned. She wasn't about to risk the same again.

A small pair of manicure scissors from her handbag did a neat job of trimming frayed edges from the cut-offs. She frowned slightly as she pulled them on and surveyed herself.

Perhaps she'd overdone it a bit. Made for someone even smaller than herself, the shorts barely covered her upper thighs, leaving the rest of her slender legs bare.

Shrugging, she decided that if her host didn't like the way she looked, he could blame himself. Donning the shirt, she rolled up the sleeves and tied the tails around her small waist.

The cream David had left for her was cool and lightly scented. She applied it liberally, rubbing it on all the exposed portions of her skin. A few swift licks with her brush were enough to smooth the tangles from her glossy black hair. She found a yellow ribbon in her purse and used that to construct a ponytail.

The result was hardly properly Bostonian, but then she wasn't in Boston. Besides, after the way she had behaved the night before, trying to project a staid, serious image was already a lost cause. Since she had nothing more to lose, she might as well relax and salvage something from what promised to be an even more difficult trip than she had anticipated.

Opening the door, she stepped out gingerly, relieved to discover that David was nowhere in sight. The cabin's outer room was as simply furnished as the one she had just left.

A couch that had seen better days shared space with an old and beautiful Navajo rug, several cluttered bookshelves, and a table with a computer set up on it. One wall was dominated by a stone fireplace, the others by uncurtained windows looking out on the desert. Through them, Julia could see a small group of people heading toward what she presumed was the dining hall.

As though in final confirmation of her restored health, her stomach rumbled. The sound startled her. She couldn't remember the last time she had felt really hungry.

Since Uncle Thaddeus's death and her assumption of his responsibilities, she had been too swamped to pay more than passing attention to her most basic needs. Meals had consisted of hurried bites of sandwiches or were more often simply forgotten.

Apparently that wasn't to be the case at Arroyo. Already the delectable aromas of frying bacon and fresh bread were making her mouth water.

Picking up her pace, she headed for the mess. The last stragglers had already disappeared inside. She could hear friendly voices exchanging morning greetings and the kind of good-natured complaining that comes with true camaraderie.

As she entered the hall and surveyed the scene, it flashed through her mind that the dozen or so men and handful of women all shared a very special vision and had committed themselves to its achievement. She felt a momentary pang of distress at the thought of the unhappiness that would result from her decision to withdraw financial support, but forced that down with a stern reminder that her responsibility to the firm came first.

Curious, guarded looks greeted her as she entered. Clearly they knew who she was. For a moment she stood at the door, feeling unexpectedly vulnerable and uncertain. Then her chin lifted and she stepped forward with a cool smile that cost her more than anyone could guess.

Or almost anyone. Across the room, David put down his coffee mug and stared at her. Even having seen her nude, her appearance stunned him. He was unprepared for her completely natural beauty, but even more he was taken aback by her undeniable youth and innocence.

Ever since finding her yesterday and learning who she was, he had kept a tight rein on his emotions. Even last night, holding her naked body against him, he had told himself she was a strong, determined woman who needed no protectors. Now he was vividly, achingly aware of having been very wrong.

A previously unexperienced emotion, some primitive combination of possessiveness and protectiveness, stirred within him. He had never known anything like it and was unsure of his ability to handle whatever it was that was happening to him.

A wry smile touched his mouth as he silently admitted the irony of his situation. After some thirty-three years free of any emotional entanglements except love for his work, he was smitten by the very woman who had the power to destroy his dreams.

Watching the fluid grace of her body as she moved toward him, he mentally acknowledged the stirring in his loins even as he decided that "smitten" was definitely the right word. It had a nice old-fashioned ring to it that suited both Julia and what she made him feel.

"What's the matter, Davey?" an amused voice next to him inquired. "Coffee bite back at you?"

Bemusedly, he focused on the weathered face of Cal Parkins, sitting next to him. The tiny woman, whose name was short for California, from whence she hailed, had passed through all the stages of life to reach an age somewhere between sixty and infinity. Salt-and-pepper hair worn in a bun framed a face bright with wise gray eyes and a ready smile.

She would have looked at home standing over a stove baking cookies for her grandchildren. But she happened to be one of the world's foremost propulsion engineers, having risen to that position despite the innumerable obstacles created by prejudice against her sex. David valued her immensely as a member of his team; he was also honored to call her his friend.

"What's that . . . ? The coffee's fine. I was just . . ." He broke off, suddenly embarrassed by the knowing glint in Cal's eyes.

"I'm not so old that I don't know what was going through your mind. That's a pretty filly."

"That filly is one very tough businesswoman. None of us had better forget that."

"She doesn't look so tough to me," Cal observed. "Looks a little scared."

That did it. David stood up swiftly, muttered some excuse, and strode toward Julia. He hadn't wanted to admit to himself that she looked uncertain about how to cope with the crowd of wary strangers, no matter how hard she was trying to hide it. But Cal's words had made him recognize what he needed to do, as much for his own sake as for Julia's.

When he reached her side, she looked up at him with surprise and, to his pleasure, gladness. His hand came to rest naturally on her shoulder as he said to the room in general, "Everyone, I'd like you to meet Julia Cabot. She'll be staying with us for a while."

Simple words, yet they held a wealth of meaning. David's tone was casual, as though her welcome was a foregone conclusion. Yet the bronzed hand on her shoulder struck a protective note that did not elude the scientists watching them. Their defensiveness gave way to relief as they were naturally led to conclude that whatever the reason for Julia's visit, relations between her and David were, at the least, good.

She flushed as she realized the implication of that. They must all know that she had spent the night in his cabin. What else did they presume? Was it expected that she had been won over to their cause in his bed?

That thought stiffened her spine. She moved away from him determinedly and forced herself to smile brightly. "It's a pleasure to meet you all. I hope my visit won't inconvenience you."

Polite murmurings assured her she would be no problem. Ruefully, she could imagine them all silently adding "so long as you don't rock the boat." Again she felt a brief spurt of sympathy for the scientists' situation, which had to be beaten down. Seeking some distraction, her gaze focused on the small, bright-eyed woman watching her.

Cal smiled gently. She held out a weathered hand and introduced herself, adding, "Don't worry about our convenience, honey. We get so tired of looking at each other, visitors are a real treat." Wickedly, she added, "Especially when they're as pretty as you. Don't you think she's pretty, Davey?"

Davey? Julia couldn't hide her grin. It was a relief to note that at least one woman wasn't overawed by the lordly master of Skyward. Of course, the fact that Cal was far older than herself took some of the pleasure out of that.

The target of her teasing question laughed good-naturedly. He was clearly used to dealing with the tiny dynamo. "Yes, she sure is, even in your clothes."

"Oh . . ." Julia glanced down uncertainly. "These are yours? I'm sorry . . . I didn't stop to think anyone might want them back." She felt suddenly terrible. Her obvious alterations of them seemed to paint her as a spoiled rich kid careless with other people's possessions.

But if that interpretation occurred to Cal, she didn't show it. "Don't you be worried about that. I told Davey you'd have to do some tailoring to make them fit. Besides—" she chuckled "—they never looked half that good on me."

"Still it was very generous of you to donate them," Julia said sincerely. "I didn't exactly come dressed for the occasion."

"First time in the desert?" Cal asked companionably as she unobtrusively steered her toward the chow line. David went with them. He decided he was hungry after all.

Breakfast was excellent. Clearly there was no stinting on food, which made sense given the austerity of their environment. Julia did full justice to a plate of *huevos rancheros*, corn muffins, thick slabs of bacon, and eye-opening coffee. Her appetite proved to be so vigorous that David couldn't resist teasing her about it.

"For a little girl," he drawled, "you sure can put it away."

She sputtered and put down her coffee cup. As loftily as circumstances permitted, she informed him, "I am not little, nor am I a girl. If you persist in believing either of those things, you'll just be setting yourself up for trouble."

Cal chuckled, then discreetly looked away. Dropping his voice so that only Julia could hear him, David murmured, "I do believe you're right. Certainly you're big enough where it counts, and as for being a girl . . . let's just say no girl ever looked as good as you."

Julia's cheeks flushed. The spurt of pleasure she felt at the knowledge that he found her attractive was smothered by anger. She suspected him of deliberately reminding her of what had passed between them in order to undermine her self-confidence.

Keeping her voice down but making no bones

about her annoyance, she said, "The fact that you've seen my body, Mr. Sherwood, is not going to make me turn tail and run. So you might as well save your breath and concentrate on answering the very hard questions I'm going to be asking."

Did she imagine a choked guffaw from Cal's direction? Not that it mattered, for David was anything but amused. His smile vanished as he met her gaze steadily.

"I don't know who put that chip on your shoulder, lady, but don't look to me to knock it off. I've got better things to do."

Before she could answer, he rose with the swift decisiveness she had already come to associate with him and walked away, pausing only long enough to exchange a few words with several of the men before disappearing out the door.

Long moments passed before she became aware of Cal watching her sympathetically. "Don't take that amiss, honey. I've always told Davey that he should have red hair instead of blond on account of his temper."

Swallowing the lump that had unexpectedly formed in her throat, Julia gratefully accepted the reassurance the older woman so gently offered. "Have you known him long?"

Cal laughed. "Seems like forever, but of course it's not. I first met Davey when he was a student at M.I.T. and I was lecturing there. In a group of very bright, ambitious people, he still managed to stand out. Not because he made any particular effort to strut his stuff. On the contrary, he was about the quietest student I've ever had."

She smiled reminiscently. "But there was something about him . . . some streak of rock-hard determination I couldn't help but recognize. I knew whatever he decided he wanted, he'd get." Her smile faded slightly as she added, "Course it was a while before I learned what had happened to him in Vietnam. He's never talked about that much, but it still marks him."

Something far more than sympathy pierced Julia as she thought of David as a prisoner of war. He was so vibrantly alive and free that confinement itself must have been torture to him. Yet he had emerged seemingly unscathed . . . or had he?

"This dream he has," she said slowly, "that private enterprise can conduct space exploration, do you really think it's possible?"

Cal took a final sip of her coffee before saying, "If I didn't, I wouldn't be here. It's not so hard these days for a woman scientist to get a good job. I've had more than my share, but when Davey called and asked me to join his team, I jumped at the chance. That boy's got hold of a comet's tail and I think he may manage a hell of a ride!"

The reference to good jobs finally shook loose an elusive memory that had been floating around in Julia's mind. Her eyes widened slightly as, for the first time, she realized fully who she was talking to. Two or three years ago, a Dr. Cal Parkins had won the Nobel Prize for science.

For several days there had been articles about her in the papers, mainly about her long struggle to win equal rights in a male-dominated field. She had succeeded brilliantly, but the battle had been long and hard. Her willingness to give up everything she had gained to follow David's dream spoke eloquently of her support for his project.

Throughout the rest of that hour, as Julia introduced herself to the members of the team, she realized Cal was not the only Nobel winner in residence. Of the eighteen people at Arroyo, four had the distinction of possessing the highest award the world could give its scientific geniuses. That was a remarkable ratio, especially given the fact that the remaining dozen looked as though they might well be candidates for the prize.

How had David managed to convince so many brilliant, seemingly sensible people to join his whimsical quest for the stars? There seemed to be only one way to find out. Taking a deep breath, she prepared for her first close-up look at Skyward, Inc.

CHAPTER FOUR

As multimillion-dollar business ventures went, it wasn't much: a collection of old cabins and rusty Quonset huts framed by wheezing generators, several battered jeeps and trucks parked near a couple of trailers that had clearly seen better days, a makeshift gantry obviously constructed of spare parts.

In this barren landscape of castoffs and debris, the rocket was a startling vision of the future. It towered some one hundred and fifty feet into the air, straight and proud, gleaming in the sun, with its red-painted nose pointed defiantly at the heavens. On one side she could make out a single word: PILGRIM.

Hardly a high-tech name, but then this wasn't a run-of-the-mill high-tech operation. As she knew from her research, the core of David Sherwood's belief in free-enterprise space exploration was his conviction that only individuals driven by personal hopes and dreams could truly take humanity to the other planets and beyond to the stars.

He argued, most persuasively, that no large, bureaucratic government agency would ever be able to accomplish a task that called for simple human courage and vision. Going even further, he asserted that if even a small part of the funding for NASA had been put in the hands of entrepreneurs, space exploration would have reached its present level of accomplishment years earlier.

To most of the space community that belief was heresy. Yet to a handful of fellow dreamers it was the stuff of legend. Staring up at the proud rocket, Julia got her first glimpse of what truly motivated these dreamers.

Always before she had thought of the "Space Race" as something outside her own life, to be viewed occasionally on television. Many of the much ballyhooed products that had resulted from it—everything from digital watches to the dehydrated breakfast drink—struck her as superfluous. While she was aware that great strides had been made in scientific understanding, she couldn't really get excited about it.

Now she knew why. She'd never before witnessed the intense determination and enthusiasm that accompanied exploration and discovery. She wondered if the air of precisely focused mental energy and heightened anticipation that she felt at Arroyo had also occurred on the voyages to the New World or at the breathless moment at Kitty Hawk.

Regardless of whether or not it had the fact remained that she doubted Skyward, Inc., could produce a profit for Cabot Venture Financing, which was after all the whole point of her firm's involvement.

It sounded so crass to bring the stuff of dreams down to hard dollars and cents, yet wasn't that how David was asking to be judged? All his talk of free enterprise would amount to nothing unless he could prove his ability to reward investors with a decent return on their money.

Shading her eyes from the intense glare of the sun, Julia looked around for him. Any ideas he might have about avoiding her should be dashed immediately. She was there for only one reason—to get information, and she meant to do that as quickly as possible.

When she found him at last, he was in the trailer that served as communications center. His tall, powerful body was bent over an oscilloscope whose screen showed a thin, undulating green line. He was frowning at it.

"Excuse me," Julia said softly, "I don't like to interrupt, but I need to talk with you."

He looked up blankly, his mind still clearly on whatever problem had engaged it. "What . . . ? Oh, all right, come on in. I'm busy right now so just have a seat and stay out of the way."

Bristling at his patronizing tone, she nonetheless managed to hold her tongue. The other men in the trailer barely glanced at her as she slid into a chair off to one side.

As they muttered over whatever it was that the

oscilloscope was revealing, Julia listened carefully. Wryly, she wondered what David would say if he realized how much of their conversation she understood.

They spoke mainly in jargon that sounded at first snatch like some arcane tongue. But thanks to her careful preparation for this trip, she was swiftly able to unravel the host of abbreviations, initials, and so on.

Apparently there was a problem with some component of the rocket booster that they were scheduled to test-fire in a few days. The problem had occurred before and they'd thought they'd solved it, but it had stubbornly cropped up again.

A large, burly man with a bristling black beard made some suggestion which the others debated. After a few minutes, they agreed to try the solution he proposed.

Julia watched with interest as David smoothly delegated authority and assigned tasks. Having only recently learned herself to be a good manager, she was able to appreciate someone who performed that function well.

He was especially skilled at getting highly intelligent people to work smoothly together. That by itself was no small accomplishment. Yet when it came to dealing with her, he seemed to vacillate between genuine friendliness and macho defensiveness.

That was pointed up yet again when the other men went off about their tasks and he at last turned to her.

Running a hand through his unruly hair, he muttered, "Sorry if you were bored. We had to get that taken care of right away."

"Of course," Julia said smoothly, "or you wouldn't have been able to test-fire the engine."

David's startlingly blue eyes narrowed. "Figured that out, did you?"

"Wasn't I supposed to?"

"Doesn't matter to me, just so long as you don't blow the problem out of proportion."

Rising, Julia strolled over to one of the trailer's grimy windows and stared out. She was silent for several moments before she looked at him again. "I'm not here to find excuses for bowing out of Skyward, David. If you can convince me this is a viable proposition, I'll be happy to continue Cabot's involvement."

Her conciliatory tone surprised them both. She hadn't meant to sound quite so amiable, and he had to rapidly reevaluate his presumption that she had arrived with her mind already made up.

"You're seriously willing to give us a chance?" he asked skeptically.

She nodded thoughtfully. "Yes, after all, unless I'm willing to take a chance on new businesses, I don't make any money. I admit that I don't understand why Uncle Thad was willing to take a shot on this, but there must have been a good reason. Why not share it with me?"

The smile he gave her stripped years off his age

and made him look suddenly like the irrepressible little boy she suspected he had once been. "I'll be glad to give you the deluxe tour," he said. "What do you say we get started now?"

"If you're not too busy . . ."

He laughed softly at her gentle reminder of his earlier attitude. As their eyes met in mutual amusement, a tremor ran through Julia. She felt as though something had touched her physically. The heightened awareness of all her senses startled her.

She was vividly conscious of even tiny details in David's appearance. His dark blond hair was a little long. It curled at the collar of his blue work shirt.

His khaki shorts were held in place by a leather belt studded with a small, beautifully worked silver and turquoise clasp. In contrast to the broad sweep of his chest, his waist and hips were narrow.

Even without her memories of the previous night, she would have known he was in peak condition. The worn running shoes he wore without socks on his long, slender feet had undoubtedly seen hard use.

Though they were standing several yards apart, she was conscious of the warmth of his skin and the almost imperceptible scent of the soap she had also used in the shower that morning. Unbidden, the image of his naked body glistening beneath the downrush of warm water flitted through her mind. She blushed and looked away.

"Shall we . . . uh . . . get started?" David suggested. He seemed equally flustered as he fumbled with the doorknob.

Outside they kept a careful distance from each other. Beginning with the labs where Skyward's basic mechanics were worked out, David took great care to explain everything that went on. As he spoke, his wariness faded and the natural enthusiasm he felt for the project came through clearly.

"We're well past the problems that plagued us at the beginning," he said. "Our first year or so was largely spent trying to figure out the essential tasks that had to be performed in order to reach our goal and then finding the people best suited to do them."

"You've put together an impressive team, if Cal Parkins and the others I met are anything to go by."

"I'm still amazed they agreed to join me," David admitted. "Our salaries are low by any standards and there's none of the perks and prestige that go with a good university or government position. Yet every time we've decided to add another person, we've been swamped with applications."

"And people say scientists aren't romantic," Julia teased gently.

"Who says that?" he demanded in mock offense.

"The universal 'they.'"

"I've been dodging that bunch all my life, and something tells me you have, too."

Julia looked up at him in surprise. "How did you figure that out?"

He shrugged disarmingly. "Simple. You're a young,

attractive woman in charge of a powerful financial company. I'm sure there are more than a few people who have let you know they think that's wrong."

It was true, but so was the fact that people rarely made that comment twice. "You make me sound positively formidable," she murmured lightly.

"Aren't you? Thaddeus would never have left you in control unless he was certain of your abilities. He was a loving man, but not one ruled by sentiment." Pausing for a moment, he looked at her appraisingly before he asked, "How old are you anyway?"

"Twenty-five," she replied, seeing no reason not to tell the truth when she already knew so much about him. The source of that knowledge was beginning to embarrass her.

Back in Boston, it had seemed perfectly reasonable to commission an investigation of him. But now that she had met the man face to face, her intrusion into his privacy embarrassed her a little.

His gaze shifted slightly, to the bare fingers of her left hand. "No commitments?"

"Not the way you mean." She spoke coolly, though she was feeling anything but. His sudden interest in her marital status was a reminder of the powerful undercurrents flowing between them. Apparently he was no more willing than she to pretend that their relationship was strictly business.

As though he felt he had ventured far enough into the personal side of her life, David shifted tack. Pointing to large stainless-steel containers set some distance away from the rest of the installation, he said, "Those hold the solid fuel we'll be using. We switched last year from liquid oxygen after our first attempt at a launch ended in an explosion on the gantry."

"That was the reason you contacted Uncle Thaddeus and asked for financing?"

David nodded. "I didn't have much choice. Practically every dollar we had went up in that blast. To rebuild and go on we needed money fast."

She couldn't ignore the hint of bitterness in his words. He was a proud man accustomed to holding what was his, yet he had been forced to turn to others for help. In exchange for it, he had yielded at least partial control of his dream.

"I know from the files that Uncle Thaddeus came out here to see you before he made his decision. Would you mind telling me how you convinced him?"

"Simple. I told him the truth. In a nutshell, what it comes down to is that space shuttle flights are pretty well booked through 1986. If you want to launch a communications satellite before then, or spend less than the two and a half million dollars NASA is charging, you have to come to us."

"Are you saying," Julia asked doubtfully, "that if you can get this to work, in effect you won't have any competition?"

David looked pleased at how quickly she had caught on. "That's it. NASA is too expensive and too busy. The other private companies working in this area are way behind us. I suppose you know about them?"

"I've heard of Ariane, the European group."

"They've done five test flights and lost two rockets. Not good odds."

"Who else is there?"

"A rather mysterious West German outfit operating in Libya, plus some government programs in Japan, India, and China."

"If it's such a good field, why aren't more people getting into it?"

Blue eyes sparkled as he laughed dryly. "Because when you say you want to launch your own rockets, you sound like a nut. Admit it, that's what you thought when you found out about us."

"Well . . . I did wonder if Uncle Thaddeus might have had too much New Mexico sun."

"Not him. He looked around here, went back to Boston, and made some phone calls. Talked to companies that are going crazy trying to find ways to launch their satellites. The simplest, fastest, most efficient way to transmit anything from a phone call to the contents of a data bank is sending it through a satellite in geostationary orbit."

"Where it circles once every twenty-four hours just like the earth so it's always over the same place."

"Right. But it takes a powerful rocket to reach that 22,300-mile height. Which is why we need so much money up front."

"Something in excess of three million dollars, to be precise," Julia noted.

"Two launches and we make it back, plus show a profit."

"How close are you to a launch?"

"A month away."

His ready answer surprised her. From the looks of the installation, she wouldn't have thought they were anywhere near that close. Her doubts must have been obvious, for David said, "Vicom International has contracted with us to launch their newest communications satellite into orbit over Washington, D.C. We expect to carry out the job four weeks from tomorrow. If we're not ready then, we'll have another chance a week later. Two missed dates and our contract is canceled."

"I see . . ." They had stopped beside the gantry holding the rocket. Julia tipped her head back almost as far as she could in order to see the top of it.

Of all the monuments humanity had created, she could think of few as impressive. Hoping her excitement wasn't overly obvious, she asked, "What exactly is involved in getting ready for the launch?"

David held up a bronzed hand, ticking off points on his fingers. "First we have to test-fire the booster engine. That's scheduled for tomorrow. Provided it goes okay, next we receive and load the satellite. After that it's simply a matter of double-checking all systems before we go."

"You make it sound not much different from an airplane flight."

"Ideally, it shouldn't be. Satellites are only the beginning. In a few years, we hope to be involved in the construction of a permanent space station. Eventually, we'll be ferrying people and materials back and forth just like a regularly scheduled airline."

"But more profitably, I hope?"

"You have the income projections in your files."

Julia nodded. Sitting at her desk in snowy Boston, the numbers had seemed preposterous. Now she wasn't so sure. The decision was turning out to be far more complicated than she had guessed.

On the one hand, her unexpected personal feelings for David predisposed her to view the venture with even more than her usual skepticism. She felt as though she needed to compensate for what she viewed as a weakness by being tougher than ever.

Yet everything he had told her suggested Skyward might be able to withstand the harshest scrutiny. Her responsibility to the firm, and to herself, demanded that she give the venture a fair evaluation.

"You're tired," he said gently. "Why don't you lie down and rest for a few hours? We'll be working out the problem with the oscilloscope, so you won't miss anything."

Though she hated to admit it, Julia did feel worn out. The ordeal of the previous day coupled with all the new and surprising emotions she was experiencing had drained her strength.

To David, who was well aware of the shadows beneath her lovely eyes, she looked like an exhausted child. At least, he preferred to think of her that way instead of as the wholly delightful, sensual woman he had held in his arms all night.

"I suppose a nap might be a good idea," she ventured, "but I can't keep using your cabin."

"Of course you can. I made room for my sleeping bag in the communications trailer."

That piece of news left her feeling oddly disappointed. Suddenly overwhelmingly conscious of her fatigue, she nodded wearily. As she opened the door to the cabin and stepped inside, she was unaware of David's gaze following her with a mixture of longing and frustration that matched her own.

CHAPTER FIVE

The sun was slanting westward and the intense heat of day had eased somewhat when Julia awoke. She lay for a while staring up at the ceiling of the cabin, trying to reorient herself from her dreams.

Sometime while she slept someone had come and draped a light cover over her. She was certain David was responsible. That simple yet intimate action made her eager to see him again.

She left the bed and showered hastily. The clothes she had worn that morning, and had fallen asleep in, were crumpled. Having rinsed them out, she hung them to dry in the shower and put on the fresh garments left for her on the table. This time there was a note attached from Cal assuring her that they were strictly surplus and to make any alterations she saw fit.

Julia gratefully took her up on that, knowing that a bit of trimming and a few tucks made all the difference. She smiled to herself as she considered that she was far more conscious of her appearance than was normal for her.

In Boston, or on any of her other business trips, she wore her "official" wardrobe and thought no more of it. But David's advent into her life had awakened a purely feminine instinct that drove her to brush her hair until it glistened and take what other measures she could to look as good as possible.

A search through the small makeup bag in her purse revealed nothing except a compact, lipstick, and a vial of perfume. With the sun warming her skin and her own thoughts softening her full mouth, the first two were unneeded. She touched a drop of the light, spicy scent behind each ear and, on impulse, in the cleft between her breasts before leaving the cabin.

That morning when David had shown her around she had been impressed by the quiet sense of purposeful activity pervading the installation. But now it seemed that something had changed. In place of the excitement and optimism she had noted before there was a new mood of tension and anxiety.

The scientists hurrying back and forth between the communications trailer and the engine booster that was to be test-fired looked grimly preoccupied. The easy camaraderie she had witnessed earlier had given way to intense concentration that suggested all the resources of the brilliant team were suddenly focused on a single problem.

David had said confidently that they would be able to solve whatever glitch had occurred with the engine booster. Was he wrong?

Quietly, so as not to disturb anyone, she stepped into the trailer. Half a dozen men were there along with David and Cal. They crouched over the instrument screens intently.

"It beats me what's wrong," a young, redheaded man muttered. "We cleared that clogged fuel line and replaced the relay switch. Everything should work."

"Should but doesn't," Cal pointed out quietly. "That engine just won't fire. My guess is we've got to strip 'er down and take 'er clear apart before we'll figure out what's wrong."

Amid a chorus of groans prompted by this remark, David straightened slowly. His mind was clearly on the problem before him, until he caught sight of Julia standing by the door. As their eyes met, some of the concern eased from him, only to be replaced by a different sort of tension.

As a pilot and astronaut, he had often been in situations where his life depended on his finely tuned, alert senses. Yet never could he remember being so acutely conscious of anything so much as he was of the woman standing rather uncertainly before him.

Despite the near-desperate magnitude of the problem facing them, he had stolen precious moments to check on her while she slept. Telling himself he was doing so only out of concern for what she had suffered in the desert, he had lingered beside the bed gazing down at her. Awake, she was a remarkably vibrant woman full of unmistakable intelligence and spirit. Asleep, she made him achingly aware of her sensuality, and her innocence.

He had left abruptly, before his instincts could override his better judgment and lead him to forget both his responsibilities and his memories.

"If I'm in the way," she said quietly, "I'll leave, but I'd prefer to stay."

He pulled out a chair for her beside him. "Sit down. You may as well get a close-up look at some of the difficulties we're encountering."

She moved with instinctive grace and sat with her hands neatly folded in her lap as though she were a schoolgirl. He grinned inwardly at the thought, only to push it aside as she crossed her shapely legs, left all but bare by her shorts.

"The booster engine?" she asked softly.

"What? Oh . . . yes. It won't fire."

"How serious is that?"

He grimaced. "Very. Without the booster, we can't lift the satellite into geostationary orbit, so there would be no point even launching it."

Hearing the worry and the weariness in his voice made Julia flinch. He mistook the cause and his mouth tightened even further. "Sorry about that, but it looks as though you may not get your money back after all."

"I wasn't thinking about the money," she insisted, hurt that he would believe she was so mercenary. Yet what reason had she given him to think otherwise?

Angry at himself for the pain he had seen flicker in

her eyes, and at her for affecting him so powerfully when he needed to be concentrating on the problem at hand, David looked away. "You have every right to be concerned," he said gruffly. "But we'll pull this out, I'm sure of it."

Swallowing her unhappiness, Julia managed to respond coolly. "If there's anything I can do . . ."

"Just do as you offered and stay out of the way." The words were harsher than he intended but their effect eluded him as he turned determinedly back to the console.

Julia observed him silently for a moment, wondering why a sensible young woman from Boston should find herself at such an impasse. For the first time in her life, she was truly attracted to a man. Yet he was totally unsuitable for her attentions.

A small, sad smile touched her mouth as she considered how very archaic her thoughts were. Men like David Sherwood hardly thought in terms of suitability. They took what they could from life and left the judgments to others.

As she studied the long, lean line of his back covered only by a thin tee shirt tucked into khaki shorts, she envied him his apparent imperturbability. Perhaps she would do well to try to copy it.

Throughout the remainder of the afternoon and far into the evening, Julia struggled to control her wayward thoughts and keep her mind firmly on the crisis confronting Skyward.

Yet as she slipped from being an observer to a

participant, she could not help but get caught up in the quietly fierce activity that had at its hub the man who fascinated her.

It seemed perfectly natural that she should keep the supply of coffee flowing to the exhausted but determined crew, cajole the crusty old cook into preparing sandwiches and soup for a stand-up meal, and otherwise do whatever she could to ease in some small way the burden on those struggling against time and odds to make the necessary repairs.

A few days before such tasks would have seemed out of keeping with her hard-won professionalism. But any such consideration of status or authority was immaterial in the face of the all-out team effort going on around her.

She lost track of the passing hours, noting only dimly that it had grown very dark and that the stars were very bright. She took a cup of coffee to David where he was stretched out beneath the engine, busily dismantling it and muttering to himself. Kneeling beside him, she touched his arm gently.

The warmth of his skin beneath her fingers made her voice husky: "Can you take a break, just for a few minutes?"

He didn't look at her as he eased out from under the engine and accepted the coffee. They sat in silence, looking at the desert shrouded in night until he said softly, "Thank you for the work you've done today."

Julia was surprised. She hadn't thought he had noticed. "It wasn't anything . . . just fetching and carrying."

"That's the point. You can't be used to doing things like that. Some people would have sat on their dignity and stayed aloof."

The image of a prissy-mouthed Miss Muffet atop her tuffet flitted through her mind. She laughed warmly. David cast a quick look at her, silently asking what the joke was.

"When I was little," she explained hesitantly, "the walls of my nursery were painted with characters from children's rhymes. For some reason, Miss Muffet in particular fascinated me. I kept waiting for her to get up and go somewhere."

He raised an eyebrow teasingly. "Who else was on the walls?"

Embarrassed at having brought up the topic, yet unwilling to retreat from a conversation that had turned unexpectedly intimate, Julia said, "Old King Cole, the blackbirds, Peter Piper . . . the usuals."

"I'll bet you had lots of toys, too?"

Actually she hadn't, but she wasn't about to explain that. Her parents had held to the view that it was wrong to spoil children, especially girls. Though they would never admit it, they had already been aware of the mistakes they had made in overindulging their eldest son. With Julia, they had gone very far in the opposite direction. Sometimes she thought too far.

"Oh . . . a few. Dolls and so on."

"What about your teddy bear?"

Her eyes widened, meeting his warily. Was it just a lucky guess or did that grin mean she had been a wee bit indiscreet? "What makes you think I had a teddy bear?" she asked.

Innocently, he parried, "Don't all little girls?"

Unconvinced, she continued to stare at him. "Did I . . . that is, last night . . . I wasn't quite myself."

His face fell in exaggerated disappointment. "Don't tell me that. You were delightful."

Her blush deepened. "But you see, that's just it, I'm not a delightful person. I'm . . . a serious businesswoman . . . with responsibilities." So why on earth did she manage to sound so forlorn, as though weighed down by a burden that was rapidly becoming too much for her?

David's expression sobered. The teasing light was gone from his eyes as he set his coffee mug on the concrete floor and regarded her gently. "Nobody's all one thing or the other. You're a mixture, just as I am. So why do I get the idea that you're fighting that?"

"I don't know what you mean . . ."

"Maybe I'm wrong, but you seem to be trying to force yourself into a mold where you don't belong." As she began to object, he went on hastily, "That's not to say you aren't a perfectly capable businesswoman. Thad was too practical and clear-eyed a man to leave you in charge unless he was sure you could handle it. But he could also be pretty arbitrary and I'll bet he never thought to ask if you wanted to take over for him."

"He knew I'd live up to my responsibilities," Julia murmured softly. She was taken aback by his understanding of her and her circumstances. Did he see everyone so clearly or was she, as she wanted to believe, somehow special to him?

"Which responsibilities? To your family or yourself?"

"My family comes first. Anything else would be selfish and immature."

David shook his head slowly. "You sound as though you're reciting something you've memorized. You can't just sacrifice yourself. If you do, you won't be any good to anyone."

"You make me sound like some sort of half-baked martyr," she objected. "Don't you think that's rather patronizing?"

"I don't mean it that way," David said, refusing to rise to the bait. He maintained an imperturbable air of patience and understanding she found oddly provoking. "What I do mean is that you have far too much going for you to feel that you have to prove yourself to anyone. You don't, not to your family or men in general, and certainly not to me."

Julia opened her mouth to tell him what she thought of that, then abruptly shut it. She wasn't sure what she thought. On the one hand, she found him presumptuous and high-handed. On the other, he made her feel good about herself in a way that was new to her.

"Look," David went on gently, "all I'm saying is

that I've been through the whole bit of living for others instead of for yourself. It doesn't work. In the end, everyone suffers. I'd hate to see you make the same mistakes I did."

Slowly, hardly aware of what she was saying, Julia murmured, "It's difficult to imagine you making mistakes at all."

David laughed, his gaze warm and gentle on her. "I've made some lulus, but I've also got a few more miles on me than you do, so I've learned a thing or two."

Looking into the light-blue eyes so full of understanding, Julia saw the truth of what he said. He had lived through experiences she could barely imagine.

His life was a testimony to the will to survive and the triumph of intelligence. For all the sorrow and suffering he'd endured, he was still able to dream gloriously.

It was something of a shock to realize how much she envied him that. Lately all her dreams had been pushed aside by the demands of the business. Sharing that moment with him in the quiet of the engine room, it came to her that she wanted to recapture those dreams. But first she had to admit them, to herself . . . and to him.

"David . . ." Her ebony hair fell across the curve of her cheek as she leaned toward him. Her lips parted slightly, her breath suddenly shallow and rapid.

He hesitated through the space of a single heartbeat before something hard and urgent coalesced within him and he gave up the struggle to resist what might never be and instead reached out for it with all the hunger of his powerful, potent nature.

The hands on her shoulders were gentle but the body she was drawn against was taut and demanding. A feminine ripple of mingled apprehension and desire darted through her. She moaned softly as her eyes fluttered closed.

What need for sight when all the other senses were magnificently alive? His mouth was warm and seeking against hers, the thrust of his tongue launching tongues of flame that spread rapidly.

She was engulfed in the driving strength of him even as her own power surged to meet his. The fine silk of his hair beneath her fingers contrasted with the rough stubble of his cheek.

She inhaled deeply, savoring the warm salty tang of a hardworking man. The pounding beat of his heart merged with the rush of blood leaping through her body.

Far in the secret recesses of her woman's spirit she was aware of immense gentleness underlying and restraining his passion. The last of her fears vanished, dissolved by instinctive trust in him.

She forgot past and future, and all the cares of the clamoring world. Nothing mattered except the moment and the man. Nothing existed except the dream.

CHAPTER SIX

It was David who at last ended the long, enthralling kiss. He drew back reluctantly, staring down at her with eyes darkened by passion and surprise. "Julia . . ."

His voice was as much a caress as his touch. She shivered helplessly, wanting nothing so much as to be close to him in every way possible.

Her hands stroked his back beneath the thin shirt, delighting in the discovery of hard muscle and taut sinew. Her breasts were pressed against his chest, her nipples full and aching.

The touch of his thigh between her soft legs made her tremble. There was no resistance left in her, only anticipation and terrible, driving need.

Fascinated, she watched the play of muscles in his throat as he swallowed tightly. Beneath his burnished tan, his high-boned cheeks were flushed. A pulse beat in the shadowed hollow of his jaw.

Pressed together as intimately as they were, she had no doubt of his arousal. With any other man, the blatant physical proof would have embarrassed her acutely. With David, she gloried in it.

Her slender body moved against his with artless grace, and devastating effect. A thick moan broke from him as his hands tightened on her shoulders and pushed her some small distance away. "Julia . . . don't! We can't . . . this is crazy . . ."

She stopped instantly, abruptly aware of her wanton behavior and stunned by it. His seeming rejection of her ripped away the haze of passion that a moment before had blinded her to any doubt or fear. With that protection gone, she knew an almost unbearable shame.

Stepping back hastily, she turned away from him, hoping he would not see the sudden rush of tears that turned her eyes to wide, shining pools of misery. "I'm sorry . . . I wasn't thinking . . ."

David sighed deeply. He felt the pain in her and did not mistake its cause. Gently his hand touched her arm. She stiffened and tried to pull away, but he would not permit it. Despite her resistance, he drew her back into the shelter of his arms.

"Let's not complicate everything further by misunderstanding each other," he murmured softly, feeling the tremors shaking her. A piercing sense of her vulnerability made his arms tighten around her. "You're a beautiful woman and you make me forget everything except what I'd like to be doing with you right now."

A shaky laugh escaped him. "Mother Nature must

have a warped sense of humor to do this to me right now." Tilting her head back, he stared down at her tenderly. "Don't you see, Julia? What's happening between us is like a chain reaction running out of control. We need to slow down just a little and get a better grip on things, or we could both get hurt."

She nodded slowly, confidence returning as the sense and sincerity of his words reached her. "I-I've never been like this. It's wonderful . . . but frightening."

"I'll say! You make me feel as though I've just ejected from a jet at fifty thousand feet and I'm falling straight through heaven."

The last of her tears fled as she laughed softly. "Thanks . . . I think."

David grinned and pressed a light kiss to her forehead. "There's a certain irony in this, you know. If I could bottle whatever's going on between us, I wouldn't have any problem getting this booster engine started."

"Maybe it just needed someone to show it how."

He wrapped an arm around her shoulder as together they glanced at the recalcitrant piece of equipment. To Julia it was no more than a jumble of mechanical parts, yet she understood perfectly well that on its performance rode the success of the entire venture.

"There has to be a solution to whatever is wrong," she said softly, "and I know you'll find it."

David squeezed her shoulder gently. A few moments before he had been feeling worn out and discouraged. Now he was revitalized, ready to tackle anything and everything to get the job done.

He didn't mistake the source of his energy. The small, lovely woman looking at him so trustingly affected him in ways he had never before experienced.

She made him feel capable of taking on any challenge, yet achingly aware of his own vulnerability. He needed her, to a degree that shocked his independent, wary nature.

For too long now he had been a loner, content with casual relationships that never touched more than the surface of his being. All his true self went into his work.

Suddenly that wasn't enough. He wanted . . . what? Things he had long ago abandoned any hope of having. A home, a family, a woman who would be at once wife, lover, friend, companion, and perhaps, someday, mother of his children.

In his desire for that kind of life he was exposing himself to danger. Could he trust Julia to accept the gift of his heart and keep it safe? Or would he end up being hurt, badly?

Without realizing that he did so, he gazed at her doubtfully. Julia recognized the look but not what had prompted it. Bewildered, she feared her newfound and very tremulous happiness was slipping beyond her grasp.

"I'd better go," she murmured. "I'm keeping you from working."

When he didn't try to stop her, she told herself that was for the best. She needed some time to consider what had happened and to try to recover her lost equanimity.

Perhaps what they had just shared was no more than a fluke brought on by tension and worry. To place too much importance on it would be to set herself up for crushing disappointment.

And yet as the long hours of the night passed and work continued, she could not forget the sensation of strong, gentle arms holding her and of a firm, male mouth that wreaked such havoc on her senses and opened a yawning pit of need deep within her.

A thousand tiny images crowded into her mind, reinforcing her fascination: David bent over the engine, his long, skilled hands adjusting the complex machinery, David talking with the crew, encouraging them despite his own worries and concern; David sitting alone, his eyes closed and deep lines of weariness etched into his face.

She wanted to go to him, to offer what little comfort she could, but she held back, fearful of the passion lurking just beneath the surface and threatening to erupt into an uncontrollable conflagration. While there was some distance between them, she could maintain some modicum of self-control. When they touched again, she would have none.

Toward dawn, David managed to identify the problem as a malfunctioning of the computer that communicated with the booster. A microprocessor that was supposed to receive the signals had failed. It took only minutes to replace what had required eighteen hours of grueling effort to find.

With that done, the decision had to be made as to whether to go ahead immediately with the test firing. The crew was exhausted, yet no one wanted to stop. Sleep was impossible until they knew for sure that the booster would work.

The long countdown continued throughout the morning and into the afternoon as all systems were checked and double-checked. Occasional halts had to be called as minor problems cropped up. Tempers were strained to the utmost, yet none snapped.

Julia did all that she could to help by seeing to it that there was plenty of warm, nourishing food, arranging cots for those who could catch a few minutes of rest, and pitching in wherever an extra pair of hands was needed.

By nightfall on the second day she was numb with fatigue. Her clothes were wrinkled, and her stomach hurt from too much coffee and too much worry.

She, like everyone else, was drawing on her final reserves of strength. The adrenaline high that had kept them going at the beginning had long since dissipated. Nothing remained except sheer determination and desperation.

Faces were tight as the final seconds ticked away. Standing in the communications trailer, Julia had a clear view of everything that was happening, but her attention focused strictly on David. He alone still looked calm and resilient, his voice never wavering as he called off the last seconds:

"Six . . . five . . . four . . . three . . . two . . . one . . . ignition . . ."

There was an instant of silence before the desert night was splintered by the roar of primal power leaping to life. The gantry shook with the force of it, yet held firm. A ball of orange light flamed outward, burning with incandescent brilliance until slowly it began to dim and finally flickered out.

The newborn silence was different from what had preceded it. It was no longer the awesome quiet of nature's empty places but the temporary curtain rung down on the first of what would be many human acts. Something fearless and magnificent had been called into being; it waited only for man to summon it again.

There was a great indrawing of breath before an exultant shout rose to the heavens.

"It works! That goddamn thing works!"

"Course it does. Didn't Davey say it would?"

"By God, we're actually going to pull this off!"

Amid all the jubilation, the shouts and laughter, the backslapping and joking, Julia stood a little off to one side. She didn't really feel part of what was happening, yet she couldn't help but share in the general elation.

Surrounded by his exuberant crew, David looked up and caught her gaze. He smiled, holding out his hand. Julia hesitated barely an instant before going to him.

Nestled into the curve of his arm, her warm, pliant body pressed against his, she felt all her weariness dissolve. In its place was a growing sense of excitement. With the successful test firing, a crucial point had been passed. What lay ahead was full of mystery, and promise.

"We've got to celebrate," one of the men declared. "I don't know about the rest of you, but I don't stand a chance of getting to sleep tonight."

"Sleep?" another inquired boisterously. "What's that? I'm ready for some foot-stomping music, some throat-charring chili, some *real* cold beer, and some *very* friendly company!"

"You're ready for Maggie's," Cal laughed. "And so's everyone else. Let's go."

"What's Maggie's?" Julia asked as she slid into the jeep next to David. Behind them the entire Skyward team was piling into trucks, pickups, anything that would roll. Headlights flashed and dust flew as they set off down the road in the general direction of the Nevada border.

"Maggie's," David laughed, "is an institution hereabouts. It's part social club and part circus. You have to see it to believe it."

A short while later, she understood what he meant.

Maggie's Place, as the glinting neon sign identified it, perched on the border between Nevada and New Mexico, smack in the middle of a major crossroads.

The large parking lot was crowded with vehicles of all description, most driven by large, boisterous men who might have stepped straight out of an earlier century.

Their mutual target was a sprawling, windowless building with fake adobe walls and a fake red-tile roof. Inside, past the double doors guarded by two very big men, Julia blinked rapidly.

The single cavernous room was dark and crowded. Scantily dressed waitresses hurried between the tables and the long bar that took up all of one wall. Up onstage, a country-music band was playing. In a cleared area in front of them, couples danced in close embrace.

It wasn't precisely what she was used to. But on the other hand, it did look like fun. With David's arm securely around her waist, she allowed herself to be guided to a table near the band. Part of the crew was already there, with the rest joining them quickly.

As orders were given for several pitchers of beer and a round of margaritas, Julia decided that come what may she was going to enjoy herself. After the exhausting two days they had all just put in, a little down-home hell-raising was definitely in order.

Which was just as well, since that was clearly what Maggie's was all about.

"I hope you like chili," David said as an entire pot of the steaming concoction arrived at the table accompanied by plates of nachos and yet another round of drinks.

"I love it," Julia assured him. She swallowed a forkful, gasped at its spiciness, and reached for her margarita. Finishing it off, she made no protest when David promptly refilled her glass.

Much later, how much she wasn't sure, she found herself on the dance floor, nestled in his arms and moving to the slow beat of a Willie Nelson tune. Her arms were wound around his neck, her breasts pressed into his chest, and her thighs cradled against his taut, hard legs. His hands rested on the jutting bones of her hips, holding her to him intimately.

"This is nice," Julia sighed. She didn't seem to be tired anymore, only rather fuzzy. After the first couple of margaritas, she had prudently stuck to beer. It didn't appear to have done any good. Her head was floating somewhere up near the ceiling and the rest of her body was going its own way, snuggled against David's.

"Glad you think so," he murmured, his teeth closing lightly on the lobe of her ear. "I wasn't sure it was your kind of place."

"I'm not stuffy," she protested.

He laughed and pulled her even closer. "No, you're not. You're sweet and thoughtful and fresh and"—his voice dropped, taking on the hint of a drawl—"quite frankly, ma'am, you pack a bigger wallop than that little ol' engine back at the base."

Giggling, Julia raised her head and made a respectable effort at batting her eyelashes. "Little ol' me? Why, sir, you must be mistaken."

One hand slipped up to cup the back of her head and his fingers tangled in her silken hair. "I don't think so, sweetheart. You're doing very dangerous things to my blood pressure."

That wasn't all, Julia thought happily. Nestled so close against him, she was vividly aware that the arousal she had felt when they had kissed that afternoon had returned in full force. David wanted her; that was unmistakable. With her customary honesty, she had to admit that she wanted him too.

But what to do about it? Nice Boston girls didn't exactly go around propositioning men. And even if they did, she was woefully lacking in the sort of experience needed to carry that off.

Through the haze of mingled fatigue and passion clouding her mind, it occurred to her that the same problem did not seem to afflict any of the other women at Maggie's. On the contrary, they didn't appear to have the slightest difficulty steering men in the direction they wanted them to go.

Even as she watched, a statuesque redhead led the way up a flight of steps with a grinning gentleman following right behind, the provocative sway of her tightly sheathed hips holding him in willing thrall.

The redhead was only one of several pretty young ladies Julia had noticed going upstairs, none alone. Even in her bemused state she had no doubt at all about what was going on up there. Maybe she and David should give it a try.

"David . . ."

"Hmmm . . ."

"Could we go upstairs?"

He stopped stock-still, staring down at her disbelievingly. "What did you say?"

"Upstairs . . ." she repeated innocently, "don't you think it would be fun?"

"Fun? Uh . . . yes . . . it would be fun . . . and other things. But I hadn't really thought . . ."

"Who needs to think? We're here to celebrate, right?"

David shook his head. He had the idea that his leg was being pulled, but he couldn't seem to mind in the least. A great wave of tenderness mingled with amusement washed over him. "Honey . . . I don't think you're in any shape to . . . uh . . . take a step like that."

Julia arched an eyebrow at him. "Oh, no? I'll have you know I can hold my miquor . . . I mean, liquor. Anyway, there's nothing going on up there except a friendly little game of cards, right?"

All but choking on the excellent imitation she was giving of a slightly daffy ingenue, he said, "Well . . . that's a possibility. Maggie does keep some rooms set aside for high-stakes players. But . . ."

"Look, there goes another couple. Let's join them."

He laughed dryly. "No, thanks. Anything more than two is a crowd."

"But there are lots more people right here . . ."

"And this is where you're going to stay," he insisted firmly.

Julia pouted mutinously. "I'll bet I could get one of the other guys to go upstairs with me."

"I don't doubt it. But if you try, I'll tan your bottom until you can't sit down for a week."

She swallowed a smile, quite pleased by the way her little ploy was working. There was no doubt that David hadn't been fooled for a moment by her silliness, but he was nonetheless responding most gratifyingly. To give him that little extra push that would send him in exactly the direction she wanted, she declared, "You can't boss me around. If I want to ask one of the guys, I'll just go right ahead and . . ."

His reaction could not have been more satisfactory. A dull flush stained his cheeks as his sense of humor abruptly vanished. Tightly, he muttered, "That does it." Hard hands whirled her around, heading her off the dance floor. Julia barely had a chance to catch her breath before she was being rapidly ushered past their table and toward the door.

Good-natured guffaws followed them out. "What's the matter, Dave, heat get too much for you?"

"Sure looks like he's in a hurry. Guess he's anxious to get to bed."

"Or something. Don't wait up for us. We'll find our own way home."

Julia opened her mouth to protest that she didn't want to leave, but then reconsidered. She had gotten what she wanted, so why push her luck. She offered no objection as he unceremoniously ushered her into the jeep, climbed in beside her, and took off down the road at a speed that made her gasp.

"Where are we going in such a hurry?" she demanded.

"Back to the base."

"Then what?"

"Then *you're* going to bed and I'm going to get my head examined."

Julia turned slightly in the seat and regarded him encouragingly. "You're not really angry at me, are you?"

A sigh of exasperation escaped him. "Of course not. It's just that things were rapidly getting out of control."

From that she concluded that he had been at least tempted to take her up on her offer. Which was good news considering her own relative inexperience. Plenty of people would say it was downright unnatural in this day and age to still be a virgin at twenty-five, yet she had nonetheless managed to prove herself not a total flop as a seductress on her very first try.

Sniffing lightly, she said, "I really don't understand why you should get all huffy. Surely I'm not the first woman who's suggested she'd like to you-know-what with you."

"No," he admitted with a wry smile, "but you're undoubtedly the first who felt compelled to refer to it by a euphemism." His tone hardened somewhat as he added, "Maybe I should have taken you up on it, after all. You were willing enough last night."

Julia blushed heatedly but refused to give him the satisfaction of admitting how discombobulated she still was by that little encounter. Summoning all her sophistication, she said, "I'm not denying that. We're both adults and we both want each other."

He cast her a skeptical look. "If I took you up on that, you'd run like a scalded cat."

Pride stiffened her spine, and fell nicely into place with all her other most basic emotions. Looking at him with far greater calmness than she felt, she said, "There's only one way to find out."

The jeep slowed as he cast her a wary look. "I'm in no mood for games."

Very deliberately, so that there could be no possibility of his mistaking her, she said, "Good, because I couldn't be more serious."

CHAPTER SEVEN

"Are you sure you really want to do this?" David asked as he followed Julia into his cabin.

Without switching on the light, she turned to face him. The remainder of the ride home had been a battle against his doubts and her own inhibitions. Having come this far, she wasn't about to give up.

That didn't mean she wasn't scared. Her legs were shaking and she guessed that she was pale, but the welcome protection of darkness would hide all that from him.

"I'd be lying if I didn't admit to being nervous," she said softly. "But I don't have any doubts."

"I must be out of my mind to even consider making love to you," he complained, running a hand through his already rumpled hair. His tone was tart and annoyed, but the light in his eyes expressed far different emotions.

A tiny surge of feminine confidence darted through Julia. She laughed softly. "That's hardly complimentary."

He took a step toward her, only to halt uncertainly. "You know what I mean. You're incredibly beautiful and you do things to me I've never experienced before. But . . ."

Julia sighed inwardly. She had never imagined it would be so difficult to seduce a man. That's what she got for finally choosing one who was scrupulous and honorable.

Slowly, so as not to startle him into withdrawing, she took his hand in hers. Looking up at him, she said, "David . . . I think you need to accept that some things in life aren't governed by logic. It's obvious that you're accustomed to always being in control of your emotions, but would it be so terrible to just let go for a change?"

His chiseled mouth quirked in a half-smile, half-grimace. "Are you sure you're willing to take the consequences of that?"

A tremor of anticipation raced through her. She swallowed tightly, never taking her eyes from his. In the quiet darkness of the room, she murmured, "Yes, I'm sure."

Three times now she had reassured him that she had no doubts. At last he allowed himself to believe. A groan broke from him as he let go of her hand to wrap his sinewy arm around her slender waist and pull her to him.

In the shadowy light, his features looked taut and hard. His eyes were hooded, but she could still see the fires burning in them.

At the first touch of his mouth on hers, Julia gasped softly. A jolt of purely sensual pleasure ripped through her. Sexual chemistry, electricity, whatever it might be called, the effect was irresistible.

She knew beyond the shadow of any doubt that she was made for this man, as he was for her. Instinctively, her soft, pliant body reached out to him, speaking in a language as old as love itself.

David had no difficulty understanding her, though the sheer perfection of what was happening between them stunned him. He groaned softly and drew back enough to look at her.

Her delicately oval face was flushed, her lips parted and moist from his kiss. Eyes like the first soft promise of dawn were half-closed, the thick fringe of lashes dusting her cheeks.

His gaze slipped lower, taking in the rapid rise and fall of her breathing beneath her thin shirt, and lower still to the narrow span of her waist, the ripe curve of her hips, and the slender legs beneath.

Remembering the beautiful body he had held naked against his own, he inhaled sharply. Part of him wanted nothing so much as to urge her down on the floor and sate himself with her at once.

But her innocence combined with his own gentleness prevented that. Somehow he had to find the strength to go slowly and make it perfect for her.

"Julia . . . I think you'd better know, I haven't been with a woman in quite a while."

Her eyes widened. "Not even the girls at Maggie's?"

"No . . . that sort of . . . encounter lost its appeal for me a long time ago."

A laugh she could no longer suppress rippled from her. She was almost giddy with happiness and anticipation. "Are you trying to tell me you don't remember how it's done?"

He stared at her for a moment, seeing the confidence she had in him and slowly letting himself believe it was justified. Reaching for her, he murmured, "Oh, I remember all right. But if I've forgotten anything, we'll discover it together."

That was fine with her, Julia thought, as he lifted her gently and strode with her into the bedroom. She felt like a bride being carried over the threshold.

In the quiet, dark bedroom they had shared once before, he set her down and stepped a little distance away. Slowly, as though savoring the moment, he raised a hand to her hair and touched it reverently.

"Your hair was the first thing I noticed about you. It was spread out on the sand, glinting like a piece of the night sky fallen to earth."

"Somehow I have the feeling that you didn't think much of me at first."

"That's not true," he corrected quietly. "I was just angry that anyone so incredibly young and lovely had endangered herself."

She shivered slightly, thinking of how close she had

come to more than simply danger. "If you hadn't found me when you did . . ."

"Don't think about that," he said quickly, drawing her to him. "You're safe and alive, with everything good ahead of you."

Julia believed him. Certainly she had never felt more secure or more vibrantly aware of herself as a woman. As for whatever was to come, she was more than willing to take each moment as it came so long as she could share them all with him.

Her fingers touched the buttons of his shirt tentatively. He stood very still, hardly breathing, as she unfastened first one, then another, and finally all of them.

Inhaling sharply, she spread the shirt open, revealing the burnished expanse of his chest. He was lean and hard, with a solid ridge of muscle extending from either side of his breastbone down over his ribs to his flat stomach. Soft curls of golden hair gave him the feel of warm fur underlaid by steel.

Hardly aware that she did so, Julia rested her cheek against him. Her arms wound around his trim waist, her thighs pressed against the hardness she yearned to discover more fully.

His hands shook as they pulled her shirt from the waistband of her shorts and slipped beneath it. Caressing the silken line of her back, he unerringly found the clasp of her bra and unfastened it.

Beneath the loose flow of material, his palms

cupped her high, full breasts, the thumbs gently kneading her taut nipples.

Julia bore it as long as she could before arching against him helplessly. "David . . . please . . . I want to be closer to you . . ."

His agreement was a husky growl followed immediately by the swift removal of her shirt. As he shrugged off his, he kept one arm around her, holding her a willing prisoner against his chest.

Trembling with need beyond any she had ever imagined, she gladly acquiesced to anything he wanted. When he unzipped her shorts and slid them down her legs, she stepped out of them eagerly, kicking her sandals off as she did so.

Naked except for the tiny scrap of cotton panty that hid little from his eyes, she asserted her own right to know him in the same way. Her hands shook as they brushed against his straining manhood, but she nonetheless managed to undo the buttons of his shorts. He stepped back for a moment, just long enough to strip off his remaining clothes, then returned to her swiftly.

She had barely an instant to savor the virile beauty of his naked form before he had lifted her onto the bed and covered her with his fully aroused length.

Julia knew a tiny spurt of fear as she felt his manhood pressing between her thighs. But David's gentle caresses soon banished that. Holding most of his weight off her, he allowed the illusion of freedom while weaving an irresistible web of captivity.

For so large a man, she thought dazedly, he was remarkably tender. Each touch of his hands, each brush of his mouth, each long, savoring stroke of his tongue was infinitely gentle yet overwhelmingly potent. Stretched out beneath him, her head tossing back and forth across the pillow, she became a creature of pure sensation unable to deny him anything.

Whatever she had read or heard about the act of love had in no way prepared her for the reality. David tuned her body as he would a fine instrument, readying her for him with tireless patience and determination.

No part of her remained untouched, no defense was left intact. When shyness forced her to try to maintain some scrap of control, he left her none.

She lost all sense of herself as someone separate from him. How could she be when their bodies entwined so intimately that she could not know precisely where one ended and the other began?

His mouth on her breasts was a sweet torment. Her nipples ached from their fullness, finding relief only in the warm, moist laving of his tongue and the rhythmic suckling that made the muscles of her abdomen clench spasmodically.

Writhing beneath him, Julia tried to return his caresses, but David would not permit it. Lightly grasping both her wrists in one hand, he laid them on the pillow above her head. "This one is for you, sweetheart," he groaned huskily. "Later we'll share."

Aware of how precarious his restraint was, she

didn't argue. Instead, she lay back and gave herself up to the incredible sensations he was provoking in her.

As his mouth left her breasts to wander down the smooth plane of her belly, his leg gently nudged hers apart. Julia guessed what he meant to do before it happened, but that did not prevent her from gasping out loud and arching upward when his teeth tenderly raked the sensitive skin of her inner thighs.

"David . . . !"

He looked up for just an instant, his teeth flashing whitely as he grinned. "Don't tell me you want me to stop, angel. I won't believe you."

Without waiting for her reply, he lowered his head again. Callused thumbs gently found and parted the folds of her womanhood. Pressing softly, he readied the most sensitive part of her to receive the homage of his mouth and tongue.

When it came, Julia cried out. Held fast in ever-tightening coils of need, she teetered on the edge of ecstasy. David let her hover there for long moments until he was at last assured that her release would be everything he wanted it to be. Only then did he part her legs further and slowly, carefully ease himself inside her.

If there was discomfort, she wasn't aware of it. Nothing reached her in the whirlpool of pleasure except an overwhelming sense of rightness. All the doubts she had nurtured over the years about the wisdom of steering clear of relationships were wiped away in that instant.

No prior experience could have made this one any better. Nor could it have come earlier. If she had met David sooner, she wouldn't have been ready for him. It had taken a certain amount of loneliness and pain to create them both. Now together they would find their reward.

The long, hard thrusts of his manhood within her increased in tempo. His features were taut, his eyes glittering as they gazed down into hers. As she felt the first undulating bursts of release, Julia's lashes fluttered down as though to shield her from his sight. But David would not permit that.

"Look at me," he grated. "I'm too much inside you to be shut out."

Mutely, she obeyed. Caught in the silver-blue fire of his gaze, she yielded the last of her defenses. As the wave took them both higher and higher, David laughed triumphantly. The citadel was his and he knew it.

But at the same instant that his conquest became undeniable, they both realized that the victory was shared. Even as the world shattered around her into an infinity of blinding joy, David was with her, as much the victim of her magic as she was of his.

Much later, when the last resonating echoes of release had given way to warm contentment, Julia stirred in his arms. She was lying half on her stomach, her head on his chest and her hair flowing over his shoulder. Her legs were entwined with his, her slender arm lying across his abdomen.

One large hand cupped the back of her head, the other rested possessively on her breast. His eyes were half-closed, but she could see the satisfaction in them, like a big, tawny cat that had hunted well.

She couldn't blame him. The experience had been shattering for her, beyond all her fantasies. If he felt some small measure of the same, she was relieved and gratified.

Propping herself up on an elbow, she gazed down at him intently. "For a man who hadn't done that in a while, you certainly have a good memory."

The deep rumble of his laughter teased her breasts. "Thanks, but frankly I can't recall it ever being like that before."

Julia wanted desperately to believe him, but she was doubtful. He was, on top of everything else, a very kind man. Naturally, he would want her to think she was truly special to him.

A vague sense of sadness settled over her. She had taken an irrevocable step which she knew she would never regret. David would always be a part of her. But life had armored her against illusions. His heart and soul were absorbed by Skyward.

What could possibly be left over for the woman who might, in the end, be forced to shatter his dream?

CHAPTER EIGHT

David was gone when Julia awoke, a source of disappointment to her since she had looked forward to being with him again. Not that they had been apart during the night. On the contrary.

Twice he had woken her with gentle caresses that led inevitably to fiery pleasure. In between, they had slept entwined, as naturally as though they had been lovers not for hours but years.

The pillow beside her still bore the imprint of his head. The clean, crisp scent of his body and the musky aroma of their lovemaking clung to the sheets. She had only to close her eyes to recapture the sense of him there with her.

Sighing, she slipped out of bed and padded into the bathroom. The shower stall was damp, but otherwise neat and tidy. She appreciated his consideration even as she wished he had awakened her to share the early morning with him.

As it was, she had slept until nearly noon, no doubt because of the exhausting two days that had gone before coupled with the unfamiliar exertions of the previous night.

By the time she finally left the cabin, after showering and dressing, the full heat of day had settled over Arroyo. The very air shimmered with it.

What little vegetation existed drooped wearily. Beyond the cluster of buildings, nothing moved. Julia thought wryly that all the animals had enough sense to lie low; only humans were foolish enough to be scampering about.

The mess tent was empty. She helped herself to a cup of coffee from the communal pot and grimaced as she drank it. After the exquisite delights of the last few hours, it was a sour comedown. Rather wistfully, she considered that peaches and cream would have been more appropriate, enjoyed in bed, of course, with David.

Speaking of whom, she wondered where he was. Over at the communications trailer, she supposed, hard at work. Finishing her coffee, she headed in that direction.

Halfway there, Cal joined up with her. "Mornin', Julia. Looks like a real nice day."

The knowing glance the older woman sent her warmed her cheeks but she managed to remain unflustered. "I hope you all had a good time at Maggie's."

"Always do, though I suspect one or two of the fellows carried on a bit more than was good for them. You and Davey were smart to leave early."

"Hmmm . . . I was just on my way to look for him. Any idea where he might be?"

"The trailer or, if not there, the booster shed." Cal clucked good-humoredly. "That boy worries over the equipment like a mother hen with her chicks."

"Can you blame him? You all looked pretty concerned before that test firing yesterday."

"We were. If that darn thing hadn't worked, we might have lost everything. But none of us has as big a stake as Davey. I swear he'd do anything to keep Skyward going."

Cal broke off abruptly, apparently aware of the implication of what she had just said. "Now I didn't mean that, really. Sure he'd do anything *businesslike* he could, but he'd draw the line at . . . uh . . . personal things."

"I know that," Julia told her quietly. Her confidence was not feigned, and yet . . . In the flood of passion that had overwhelmed them both the previous night, she had tossed her usual caution aside and resolved to live for the moment. In the bright light of morning, she had to admit that might have been a mistake.

David was only human, as she had discovered so delightfully. Skyward was far more than simply a business venture to him. It was his declaration of independence, his dream of what individuals could achieve, his vision of the future.

How could any man hope to separate such powerful motivations from his personal life? And how could he be expected to ignore any possible advantage that might help him gain what he so desperately needed?

Without the continued support of Cabot Venture Financing, Skyward would most likely fail. Had David, even subconsciously, decided to do everything he could to assure her firm's continued support?

The mere thought made Julia cringe inside. But she showed no sign of what she was feeling as she left Cal and continued on her way toward the trailer. Entering it, she was surprised not to find the usual cluster of scientists. Only David was seated in front of the control console, studying the wavering lines as they danced across the screens.

Julia stared at him longingly. So caught up was he in his work that he had not heard her come in. She was free to observe him unawares.

An unruly strand of sun-bleached hair fell across his broad forehead. His eyes were half-closed in concentration, his lips set firmly. The khaki shirt and shorts he wore were almost identical to those he had had on the day before. She remembered watching him take them off, and flushed.

Clearing her throat discreetly, she drew his attention to her presence. He looked up blankly, only to stiffen when he saw her.

"Uh . . . good morning . . . afternoon, actually," he murmured. "Is there something I can do for you?"

Julia frowned. This was hardly the kind of greeting

a woman expected from her lover. She took a step toward him, only to stop when he stood up and moved away. He didn't precisely turn his back on her, but after that first quick glance, his eyes were averted and he appeared very distracted.

Her throat tightened. Was he so sure of her now that he thought he no longer even had to be polite?

"I just wanted to see how everything is going." That wasn't true, but it was as close as she was willing to get to admitting how much the mere sight of him meant to her.

"Everything is fine," he said brusquely. "I can understand why you're concerned, but after yesterday's successful test, you should feel less worried about your investment."

Julia's lips parted soundlessly. She couldn't believe he had said that. It seemed to reconfirm her deepest fears. Where was the sensitive, understanding man of the night before? In his place, she could find only a stranger whose motives were suddenly highly suspect.

"I'm not worrying about my investment," she told him stiffly. Spurred by the hurt he had so easily inflicted, she added, "Worrying doesn't do any good. You'll either succeed with the launch or fail, and I'll make my judgment accordingly."

Some portion of her bitterness must have reached him for he sighed heavily. "Julia . . . about last night . . ."

She waited, hoping he would say something, anything, to soothe over the damage he had done and restore the heady happiness she had been feeling only moments before. But instead he looked away from her again.

"We were both exhausted," he muttered, "and not really in control of ourselves. I should never . . ."

"You don't have to say anything more. I get the point."

Though she tried valiantly to conceal it, the anguish his words caused her could not be completely hidden. Her eyes were clouded with unshed tears as she turned blindly toward the door.

Her hand was on the catch when David moved. He crossed the small distance in rapid strides, his lean, burnished fingers closing around hers. "Julia . . . I'm putting this very badly . . ."

She had to get out of there. Another moment and she was going to disgrace herself. "It doesn't matter," she assured him shakily. "I'll just chalk it up to experience." A bitter laugh escaped her. "Lord knows I can use some of that."

"Don't talk like that!" Though she struggled against his hold, he refused to release her. Instead, his arms wrapped around her gently but firmly.

She held herself stiffly in his embrace, refusing to give him the satisfaction of struggling. His strength was a source of resentment, as was the ease with which he could control her and the terrible vulnerability he made her feel.

For so long she had been plagued by doubts about

herself and her ability to cope with all the demands placed on her. For a brief period he had made her forget her fears and believe that anything she truly wanted was possible. It would have been far kinder not to have given her that glimpse of happiness only to rip it away.

"I can hear the wheels going around in your head," he said wryly, still holding onto her. "Whatever you're thinking, it's wrong."

"Thanks," she muttered, refusing to look at him despite the gentle persuasion of his fingers under her chin. "It's so nice to know that you find me transparent *and* foolish."

Giving up the effort to raise her head, he pressed it to his chest and rocked her gently. "You're a bundle of contradictions. Part tough businesswoman, part winsome child." A soft laugh broke from him. "And all woman."

Pressing a light kiss to the top of her head, he said firmly, "There is no way I'm letting you leave here until we get this straightened out. I'm sorry I acted like an insensitive boor just now, but what happened last night really shook me up. I was afraid I'd rushed you and that once you'd had a chance to think things over, you'd want me to go straight to the devil."

Her head lifted warily as she peered at him through thick lashes stiffened by unshed tears. "Afraid? You?"

David nodded ruefully. "Scared to death. I woke up this morning and lay there looking at you, knowing I'd never seen anything so beautiful and desirable. It was all I could do not to make love with you again."

"Why didn't you?"

The question burst from her in such innocent candor that he couldn't help but laugh. "Because I thought I might already have done our relationship a lot of damage and I didn't want to make things worse." Meeting her eyes, he went on quietly, "It's not as though we'd met in some ordinary way with no complications. You have a decision to make about Skyward. Personal involvement will only make that tougher."

"I agree with what you're saying," Julia acknowledged, "at least in theory. But the fact is that we are involved, very personally."

"And that's what I regret." David sighed. Swiftly, he added, "Only in terms of timing. I wish we had waited until this whole matter of Skyward's funding was settled."

Hesitantly, she asked, "Do you really think we can separate one from the other?"

"No . . . not until you make up your mind."

"But I can't do that until after the launch."

"I know, which is why I think maybe we'd better put some distance between us." Even as he spoke, he was gently easing her away. His hands fell at his sides, leaving only his eyes touching her.

"Believe me, this is the toughest thing I've done in a long time. But I'm convinced it's for the best. After the launch, we'll have plenty of time to concentrate on each other, and there won't be any complications to muck things up."

Julia stared at him perplexedly. She was swept by contrary emotions. His seeming determination to look out for her interests at all costs should have reassured her about his true feelings for her.

But instead she was left wondering if their intimacy wasn't being used almost as a carrot to prod her into deciding in Skyward's favor. That was a harsh yet unavoidable thought.

David might have been out of practice for a while, but he could not possibly be unaware of how totally she had responded to his lovemaking. The realization that her body had no secrets from him made her feel piercingly exposed and defenseless.

What he was saying to her in essence was that they wouldn't make love again until she made up her mind about Skyward. And if she decided against it, realistically what possible hope was there that their relationship would resume?

Hurt though she was by the direction of her thoughts, Julia could not blame David. With so much at stake for him, he might not even be conscious of what he was doing. He was, after all, a survivor who had learned in a harsh school how to protect himself.

Softly, he broke in on her thoughts. "Do you understand why I feel we have to do this?"

She nodded, unable to speak until she had swallowed against the dryness of her throat. The impulse to try to argue with him was so strong within her that she had to struggle against it.

"I think so . . ." she said at length. "I'm just not sure you do."

He frowned. "What do you mean?"

The last thing she wanted was to get into a discussion with him about the state of his subconscious. No matter what either of them might say, she would sound as though she were trying to persuade him to continue what they had begun the night before. Her pride would never permit that.

"Never mind," she murmured, stepping toward the door and opening it. "If we're going to stick to your plan, I'd better clear my things out of your cabin."

"No, I want you to stay there."

His swift objection surprised her. She hesitated for a moment before reason asserted itself. "Be sensible, you can't work as hard as you are and sleep on the floor someplace. I'll ask Cal if I can bunk with her."

"She has a weird sleep schedule, only a couple of hours at a time. You'd never get any rest."

"Then I'll do what you were doing and use a sleeping bag."

He shook his head vehemently. "I won't hear of it. You went through a terrifying experience only a few days ago and you need plenty of rest."

Baffled as to why he should be stubborn about this, she tried to make him see reason. "This is silly. I'm perfectly capable of roughing it for a few nights."

David brushed that aside without a flicker. "If you try to move out of my cabin," he informed her succinctly, "I'll move you right back in."

The grim set of his mouth and the hard glitter of his eyes told her he was serious. For some reason she couldn't fathom, he was determined to keep her where he had decided she should be. Two could play that game.

"All right . . . I'll stay in the cabin, but only on one condition."

He raised an eyebrow warily. "What's that?"

"You sleep on the couch in the other room."

"That is not going to help the situation any."

"I don't care," she said flatly. "That's the deal. Otherwise, forget it."

David stared at her for a moment, taking in the defiant set of her chin and the steadiness of her gaze. Slowly some of the tension eased from him, replaced by tender amusement. Quietly, he said, "You're very stubborn."

She sniffed disparagingly. "Talk about the pot calling the kettle black . . ."

"I still meant what I said about keeping our distance."

"I know you did. What do you think, that I'll creep out of bed at night and attack you?"

"Actually . . . that might be fun." At her reproving look, he quickly added, "Just kidding. All right, you've got a deal."

Julia nodded, satisfied that she had won that round.

She left feeling more cheerful. David could come up with all the plans he liked. But she had something to do with how their relationship turned out, and she didn't intend to let him forget it.

CHAPTER NINE

Julia's good humor lasted only until she discovered that David had meant what he said about not making love again until the issue of Skyward's future was decided.

In the back of her mind, she had known he was a strong, decisive man who, once having made up his mind to do something, would not be easily swayed. But she hadn't quite been prepared for the consequences of that.

Lying alone in the bedroom that night, achingly aware of him only a few feet away on the other side of the door, she had felt a definite spurt of feminine pique. Having been once aroused to her full potential as a woman, it was rather frustrating to have to damp down her feminine yearnings even temporarily.

Morning saw little improvement. David was courteous but aloof. The VICOM satellite was due to arrive that afternoon and all his attention was focused on the final preparations needed to ready the rocket to receive it.

Although everyone seemed genuinely appreciative of her efforts to help out wherever she could and her willingness to do jobs they would have expected her to find beneath her, Julia felt very much like a fifth wheel. It was Cal who finally noticed her discomfort and proposed a solution.

"Honey," the scientist said kindly, "I think you're suffering from a too intensive dose of Skyward. It happens to the best of us, especially when the pressure gets really bad. So, if you wouldn't mind, maybe you could do yourself a favor and help all the rest of us out by running a few errands in town."

"Town?" Julia repeated, surprised. "I didn't know there was one."

Cal chuckled. "It's more of a wide spot in the road 'bout five miles from here. But there is a general store and post office."

"Sounds good to me. I'll collect lists of whatever everyone needs."

An hour later she had accepted the grateful thanks of the crew, along with their lists, and set off. Her rented car had been picked up by the agency and towed away for repair of a ruptured fuel line. She had declined the offer of a replacement.

The battered jeep she borrowed made her feel a lot safer. Nonetheless, she was careful to leave word of her time of departure, her route, and when she expected to be back. That was a strict rule David had established when the base first came into existence.

Cal's "wide spot in the road" turned out to be

exactly that. A rickety old building that looked as though it had been there since the Flood perched beside a parking lot empty of all but a few other vehicles similar to her own.

Inside, she found all the trappings of another era, from the sawdust-strewn floor to the shelves piled high with paisley cloth, pots and pans, canned goods, and huge sacks of flour. A grizzled miner complete with a pickax dangling from his belt was hard at work playing checkers with the proprietor.

"Jus' a sec', Ezekiah," the slightly younger gentleman with a bald pate and a rotund tummy said when he caught sight of Julia. Rising, he smiled a welcome. "Can I help you, little lady?"

Swallowing her smile at the appellation that made her feel as though she had stepped into a Wild West movie, she nodded. "I hope so. I've got a list of supplies the people out at Arroyo need."

"Well now that figures, seeing as how none of 'em has been in lately. Guess they're pretty busy out there."

Julia agreed, but said little more. She appreciated a friendly chat as much as the next person, but when it came to speculative business ventures she had learned to hold her tongue and impart as little information as she could.

The two gentlemen didn't seem to want for information as it was. Sticking the stub of an unlit cigar in his mouth, the miner said, "They must be about ready to shoot that thing off. I sure hope I don't miss seeing it."

"Don't see how you could," said the store owner. "It figures to make one hell of a noise, begging your pardon, miss."

"Gonna put a satellite in orbit, they say. Seems like that's been going on for quite a while now. Don't see what all the fuss is about."

"That's 'cause you haven't been listening too good, Ezekiah. This is the first time folks tried to do it on their own without the government running the show."

"Never have thought much of the government. Keep sending me forms and stuff to fill out."

"You still throwing those away?"

"Don't see what else I can do with 'em, Jeb. You know I don't write real good what with my arthritis and all."

"You do okay with those letters to that widow over at River Gulch."

The old miner shrugged dismissively. "Man's got to have some incentive." He thought for a moment, then added, "I guess that's what those folks out at Arroyo are all about. They got an idea in their heads and they just won't rest till they make it work. You gotta admire that kind of gumption."

"Just so long as they don't blow nothing up they aren't supposed to," Jeb murmured.

"I don't think there's any danger of that," Julia said dryly. "They're being very careful."

"That's good." Jeb began filling a bag with the items she had picked out. "That guy running things out there, Sherwood, he strikes me as a man who knows his own mind."

"I talked to him a while back when he first came out here," Ezekiah said as he obligingly lifted a bag of flour the cook wanted. "He'd been over there in Vietnam. Didn't say much about it but I got the feeling he'd been looking for something to make up for it ever since."

"My nephew's the same way," Jeb acknowledged as he totaled the bill. "Took him a few years to settle down from that, but now he's got a good life. Works harder, though, than just about any man I know. Seems like he's got to build something to kind of balance out all the destruction he saw."

"Wasn't like that after the Big Number Two, was it, Jeb? We came back right proud of ourselves."

"So was everyone else. Nobody questioned what we'd done. Those boys who went over to 'Nam had it a lot worse."

Julia listened silently as the men reminisced about their own experiences in World War II and the much later and different war that had swept up another generation. She thought back over what she knew of David's life since his release as a prisoner of war.

Everything he had done—from his entry into M.I.T. to his departure from NASA—could be interpreted as a carefully thought-out plan leading him directly to Skyward. If that were true, then the dream had taken hold of him when all else must have seemed gone beyond recovery. No wonder he clung to it so tenaciously.

Having filled the crew's shopping lists, she set about seeing to her own needs, her mind still absorbed by thoughts of the remarkable man whose life she was suddenly sharing.

Cal's kindness notwithstanding, she had begun to feel the limitations of her wardrobe. That was quickly remedied by purchasing several shirts and pairs of shorts similar to those everyone else at the base wore, plus jeans for the cooler nights. Far in the back of a shelf, she discovered several sets of "baby doll" pajamas and on impulse added them to her bundle.

With Jeb and Ezekiah's help, she got everything loaded into the car, including the bundles of mail she had picked up. Only one other chore remained to be done. As long as it was on her mind, she might as well make the phone calls she had been putting off.

"Do you have a pay phone I can use?" she asked as she returned to the store to settle her bill.

"Sure thing, miss. Right over there." Jeb directed her to a corner in the back. Using her credit card, she was quickly put through to her office.

Her secretary, Catherine, answered the phone, and in response to her inquiry assured her that everything was running smoothly. "We're all fine here, Ms. Cabot. The contracts came through on the real estate deal and your banker called to confirm the financial arrangements you had requested. On those oil-well leasing negotiations, your bid has been accepted. I'm putting the paperwork through right now. It should be ready by the time you get back."

"That's good, though I'm not absolutely clear on how much longer I'll be here."

"Is there some problem?" Catherine asked.

"No . . . not exactly. The first launch is scheduled for a few days from now and I don't want to miss it."

"I don't blame you. It must be tremendously exciting." As though recalling that her employer wasn't too enthusiastic about the project, she added, "I mean just theoretically, of course. It's not as though it were practical."

"That remains to be seen. I'll keep in touch. If anything comes up, give me a call." She hung up a moment later, shaking her head at how ready she had been to spring to Skyward's defense. Catherine's very mild criticism had provoked a sharply defensive response. If David felt any measure of the same, and he must, he had treated her very gently indeed.

But then he was a gentle man, as she had every reason to know. Gentle, strong, passionate . . . Muttering to herself, she reined in her thoughts. This would not do. She had one more call to make and wanted to get it over with as quickly as possible.

"Hello, Mrs. Wilkerson. Is Mother in?"

"I'm afraid not, miss. She's at a committee meeting."

The relief she felt at being let off the hook made

her feel faintly guilty. "Would you tell her I called? I'll try to get back to her later."

Having ascertained that the redoubtable housekeeper would pass on her message, Julia hung up. Had her relationship with her mother been different, she could have confided in her about David and asked her advice. But that was impossible. Wistfully, she wondered what it would be like to have the loving, attentive kind of mother so many people took for granted in their lives.

Only Uncle Thad had shown a loving interest in her, and even he had expected her to conform to his wishes, never thinking that she might not want to take charge of the family business.

Only David seemed willing to give her the room she needed to be herself. Or did he? She still couldn't shake the nagging fear that his determination to keep some distance between them was a ploy to assure that she decided in Skyward's favor.

The trip back to base seemed longer than on the way out. She was tired and thirsty by the time she pulled up beside the corrugated metal motor pool and began unloading her bundles.

Her thin tee shirt stuck to her and perspiration matted her hair when she finally deposited the last package in its owner's trailer and wearily made her way to David's cabin. There was no sign of him, as usual. He had been gone before she awoke that morning and she had no doubt he would be turning in late.

Peeling off her clothes, she headed for the shower. The tepid water cooled her overheated body and revived her spirits. She shampooed her hair and was rinsing it when the door suddenly opened.

A large, burnished hand abruptly pushed aside the curtain as David demanded, "Are you all right? Why didn't you answer me?"

Acutely aware of her nudity, she looked around for something to cover herself with only to discover that the towels were out of reach. "A-answer you?"

"I called to you when I came in and heard the water running. When you didn't say anything, I thought you might have gotten dizzy or something and fallen." As he spoke, the tenor of his voice changed. Anxiety mingled with annoyance gave way to a far different sort of tension.

His eyes ran over her hungrily, taking in the slender line of her body, from her glistening hair down past her high, firm breasts to the slim curve of her waist and the flair of her hips below.

Under his gaze, she flushed. There was no doubt that David found her beautiful, and very desirable. That knowledge warmed her, even as it made her acutely aware of her own need for him.

His shirt hung open, baring the broad expanse of smoothly muscled skin dusted by golden hairs. She remembered the feel of him beneath her hands, against her breasts, and trembled.

"Julia . . ." he muttered thickly and took a step closer to her, only to think better of it. His hands dropped to his sides as he hastily glanced around. Spying the towels, he seized one and wrapped it firmly around her.

His hands were roughly gentle on her skin as he dried her. She stood quietly for his ministrations, not wanting to do anything that would puncture the sudden closeness between them. As he finished and picked up her robe, the towel fell away from her, revealing the glowing length of her all pink and soft, with her nipples taut from his touch.

He stared at them for what seemed like a long time before he groaned deep in his throat. Under any other circumstances, the fierce glitter in his eyes would have frightened her. He looked like a dangerous predator determined to show no mercy to his prey.

But this was David, the man with whom she had shared the ultimate in ecstasy. She had held him in her arms as he shook with the force of his own release and had felt his vulnerability to the core of her being. No matter what doubts might still lie between them, she could not fear him.

An infinitely feminine smile curved her mouth as she began to open her arms and reach out to him. But a sudden thought made her freeze.

She could persuade him to make love to her, of that she had no doubt. But what would be her true motive for doing so? To prove that she could make him want her more even than he wanted the funding for Skyward?

The thought that their joining could be tainted by all that lay between them made her feel hollow inside. She could not bear that. The beauty they had found together must be kept above all the other concerns that plagued them.

The pain in his silver-blue eyes told her that he thought so, too, but that for the moment at least he would not be able to overcome his desire for her unless she helped.

Reluctantly, fighting the desperate urges of her body, she took the robe from him and put it on.

CHAPTER TEN

The VICOM satellite arrived the next morning, accompanied by several representatives from the company, including Alex Wilshire, the vice-president of systems engineering. He was a short, balding man of about fifty who held himself ramrod straight in an effort to overcome his deficiency in height and whose sharp features were set in a perpetual frown.

Accompanying him were three younger men—all dressed like him in short-sleeved white shirts and plaid knit slacks—who said nothing except to agree with him and who seemed to have no higher interest in life than avoiding his wrath.

As Julia showed him around the installation—a duty she had volunteered for since everyone else was so busy—Wilshire paid scant attention to what she had to say. As she began to describe the various buildings and their functions, he broke in abrasively:

"NASA makes this place look like a Tinker Toy. The mere thought of trusting you people with our bird ties my stomach in knots."

Julia frowned. She guessed he was trying to knock her off balance, to establish some sense of weakness that could be used to his advantage.

The technique had been tried on her before and she knew herself to be immune. But that didn't lessen her annoyance.

Calmly, giving no hint of her thoughts, she asked, "Then why are you?"

Her failure to rise to the bait made him scowl. "Because," he snapped, "Sherwood made such a persuasive case for himself that we decided to give him a try. Now I'm having second thoughts."

"Really?" Julia smiled skeptically. "That's surprising considering the difficult position VICOM is in because of its failure to adequately anticipate both its customers' requirements and the aggressiveness of its competitors. It seems to me that with the ground you've been losing lately, you should be grateful for Skyward's existence. It's your only chance to recover and move ahead."

Wilshire's face reddened. He wasn't accustomed to anyone challenging him so openly, much less an attractive young woman. His three assistants glanced at each other anxiously. By unspoken accord, they withdrew slightly.

"Have you got any idea what kind of insurance premiums we're paying?" Wilshire demanded.

"I suppose they're higher than usual, but that's to be expected."

"Maybe by you. But I'm worried. Our estimated

return-on-investment for this little jaunt is not what it should be."

Unimpressed, Julia shrugged. "Then why did you agree to Skyward's terms if you don't think you'll get your money's worth?"

"I told you, it seemed like a good idea at the time. If I had my way, we'd reopen negotiations with Sherwood to improve our position."

Recognizing a tentative feeler when she heard one, she wasted no time slapping it down hard. "It's too late for that."

Wilshire laughed dryly. "I'm not so sure. It's not as though people are lined up to do business with him."

Beneath her calm demeanor, Julia was seething. She knew that such ploys were not unusual in business, but that didn't make them any more pleasant to swallow. "Let me give you a piece of advice," she said quietly. "David Sherwood is not a man to cross. If you try to push him too far, he'll shove back twice as hard. You could find yourself with a very expensive satellite and no way to launch it."

Wilshire smirked, unconvinced. "Are you really trying to tell me that as the major financial backer for Skyward, you would allow him to cancel his contract with us for any reason?"

"Yes, that's exactly what I'm telling you. Any idea you have about this being a shaky venture desperate for customers is sadly mistaken. I'll back Skyward—and David Sherwood—one hundred percent." Her vehemence surprised her but she managed to conceal that. Not for nothing had she faced tougher men than Wilshire across the bargaining table.

The vice-president glared at her. His confidence in his ability to manipulate her was fading fast, but he still wasn't quite ready to give up. "I suppose you have to say that, though I can't figure out exactly why. Isn't this just some kind of tax shelter for you?"

Julia wasn't about to fall for that one. Her violet eyes were coolly direct as she said, "Cabot Venture Financing doesn't waste its time with unprofitable businesses just to get tax write-offs. We go where we see profit. It's as simple as that."

"Is it, Ms. Cabot?" Intimidation having failed, Wilshire switched to scorn. "Frankly, I was astonished when I found out that your firm is footing the bill for this venture."

"Oh? Why was that?"

"Come on, it's obvious. Cabot has a reputation for being a solid, level-headed company. This just isn't your cup of tea. Of course, now that I've seen the situation for myself . . ." He let his words trail off meaningfully.

Julia bridled inwardly. She had the sinking feeling that she knew exactly what he was thinking, but still felt driven to confirm it. "What, precisely, are you getting at, Mr. Wilshire?"

"Just that now that I've seen you and Sherwood I understand how all this happened." He laughed coldly. "Far be it from me to get in the way of true love, Ms. Cabot, but I must say, your professionalism leaves something to be desired."

What could she say to him? No man reached his position without a fair degree of perceptiveness. He was right, on all counts. Yet he was terribly, totally wrong.

Taking a deep breath, Julia willed herself to stay calm. "Mr. Wilshire, the last thing I want is any unpleasantness with a Skyward client, but I must tell you that you are out of line. My relationship with Mr. Sherwood, *whatever* that amounts to, is none of your business. All you need to be concerned about is the fact that Skyward will do an excellent job of launching your satellite."

He looked unconvinced, but unsure of what to say next. Lacking real ammunition, he had to settle for vague threats. "I hope you're right, Ms. Cabot. If you aren't, it will be tough enough on VICOM but we'll manage. You and Sherwood, on the other hand, will be in for a hell of a rough time."

Julia didn't reply. She knew he had no real idea of how right he was. Far more than he could ever have guessed was riding on the successful launch of Pilgrim and its cargo. With it would go all her hopes for a future that was beyond the understanding of a man like Wilshire.

By midafternoon, the satellite had been checked out to confirm it had suffered no damage in transit and was ready for transfer to the rocket. The metallic cylinder was less than six feet long and weighed only a few hundred pounds. Yet maneuvering it into position above the boosters was a backbreaking effort requiring hours of painstaking work.

The most experienced crane operator David had been able to find slowly hoisted the delicate package into the air. As the scientists and the VICOM representatives watched from the ground, it was cautiously inched toward the side of the rocket.

Julia held her breath as the cylinder swayed back and forth, dangling from the metal cable that was all that kept it from smashing to the ground. Even the slightest bump could severely damage the delicate mechanism.

Beside her David appeared outwardly calm, but she could sense the tension radiating from him. Instinctively, her hand reached for his. He glanced down at her and smiled gently. Apprehension made way for a rush of pleasure that stayed with her through the final moments of the critical maneuver.

When the satellite was at last within reach of the technicians poised on the gantry, they carefully tugged and nudged it into the steel cradle atop the boosters. If all went well, it would remain there until being jettisoned into orbit.

A cheer went up from the relieved crew, but their celebration was brief. There was still an immense amount of work to do. Darkness fell with its usual abruptness and strings of bright lights were turned on, transforming the gantry and rocket into a giant's Christmas tree.

The desert night was starkly clear. Julia knew enough about navigation from her sailing days to be able to recognize many of the constellations. Lovely Andromeda had risen in the east with Pegasus prancing nearby. The glowing beauty of Cassiopeia lit up the great swathe of the Milky Way, rivaled only by the brilliance of Vega.

The moon was little more than a sliver but Saturn shone so clearly she could almost fancy she could see the rings. Venus, wreathed in mystery, hugged the westward horizon. Mars, bathed in red, glistened enigmatically.

The night grew old but still the work continued. Every pressure gauge and voltage meter was checked and double-checked, as were the on-board computers that would carry the vital launch commands and ultimately deploy the satellite itself.

The twins, Castor and Pollux, climbed higher in the sky, forever chasing Taurus. Southward, Orion hunted, the three jewels of his belt winking brightly.

A falling star, skimming earthward like a pebble to a pond, caught Julia's eye. Childlike, she whispered a wish on the cool desert wind.

The need for sleep became irresistible. She checked the coffee supply one last time, spread blankets over the crew members who were managing to nap, then made her solitary way to the cabin.

Lying awake in bed, she watched the glow of artificial light showing through the curtains and thought of David. They had spoken almost not at all that day, yet they had been close in a way that needed no words.

The intimacy of shared glances, private smiles, the swift touch of a hand or the caressing note of a voice was a kind of lovemaking she had never guessed existed. But far from satisfying, it merely whetted her appetite for more.

With the restraint of other eyes removed, the fire she had barely kept banked all day began to flare to life. A soft groan broke from her as she twisted on the sheets, wanting him so badly that she ached from it.

Patience, never her strongest suit, eluded her. She sought sleep as an escape, only to drift through uneasy visions of shattered stars and worlds careening out of control.

She woke suddenly in the gray time before dawn to the sound of someone entering the cabin. David's steps were already as familiar to her as her own, but even if she had not been able to recognize them, she would have simply known he was near. His presence subtly altered her surroundings, making her at once more content and more restive.

She waited until she heard the couch sag under his weight. Leaving the bed, she hesitated a moment before easing the door open.

He was sitting on the edge, his elbows resting on his knees and his head in his hands. Though she could not see his face, she knew he was exhausted. There was a tension about him that warned her that he was precariously close to his limits.

Swiftly, without pausing to think of the consequences, she went to him and knelt on the floor at his feet. Her hands reached for his even as he looked up, startled.

"Julia . . . I'm sorry . . . I didn't mean to disturb you."

"That doesn't matter. What's wrong? Has something happened?"

For an instant she feared he would make another remark about her concern for her investment, but he did not. Instead, he shook his head wearily and touched a gentle hand to the curve of her cheek.

"No, as far as we can tell, everything's fine. Launch is scheduled for five hours from now."

"Then you must get some rest."

"I suppose," he agreed reluctantly. At her gentle urging, he lay down on the couch. She thought he would let her go, but instead found herself being drawn down with him.

When she stiffened slightly and made to pull away, his taut thigh moved over her legs to gently trap her as he murmured huskily, "Stay with me, beautiful Julia. I don't want to be alone tonight."

Her throat tightened as she ceased her efforts. This, at least, she could do for him. With so much else in doubt, how could she refuse?

"Are you sure," she asked when they were stretched out together side by side, "that nothing is wrong?"

"We went over the checklist again and again. It all works like a charm."

"Then why are you . . . ?"

"Worried?" He laughed faintly, mocking himself. "I don't know. That's the hell of it. I just can't shake the feeling that something is out of kilter."

Held snugly against him with her head on his broad chest and the rhythm of his heartbeat accelerating the pace of her own, she resisted the idea that all was not right. "If there was a problem, wouldn't it have shown up by now?"

"I'd sure like to think so, but with a system this complex it's hard to tell. We didn't know there was anything wrong with the rocket booster until we tried to test-fire it."

"But that was the whole point. You tested it to make sure it worked. When it didn't, you fixed it. Hasn't everything to do with the rocket been thoroughly analyzed?"

She felt the low rumble of his weary laugh. "To the point where we're all ready to drop. And yet . . ." His voice trailed off and for a moment she thought he might have fallen asleep. But when she tried to move away, his arms tightened around her instantly. "Are you uncomfortable?"

"No, it's just that . . . this couch is a little narrow." Propping herself up, she gazed down at him gently. "May I suggest that we adjourn to the bedroom?"

David hesitated, obviously torn between his resolve not to succumb to his desire for her and his need for the simple comfort of her nearness. Seeing the conflict within him, Julia smiled tenderly. "If you'll come to bed with me, I promise not to try to take advantage of you."

He shot her a grateful look as he fell in with her teasing. "That's what all you women say."

"And I suppose you'd know," she muttered dryly.

"Only because my mother told me," he claimed as they rose together and headed for the bedroom. His arm was around her shoulders, hers embraced his waist. She could feel the weariness in his every step and was more determined than ever that no matter what worries plagued him he was going to rest.

Easing him onto the bed, she bent down and slipped off his shoes. He mumbled some protest, which she ignored as she slid his shirt free of his waistband and gently tugged it over his head.

His bare chest held her spellbound for a moment before she recollected herself enough to say, "Stand up and let me finish undressing you."

He obeyed without further objection, stepping out of his shorts and briefs before dropping back down on the bed. She tried to keep her eyes averted, but his nudity was a compulsion she could not ignore.

Everything about him—from the top of his sunburnished head clear down the length of his magnificently masculine body—called to her. He looked like a proud, untamed animal capable of both majestic nobility and ruthless savagery.

Yet in the final analysis, he was simply a man, tired, worried, and in need of all the comfort she could give.

Stretching out full length, he groaned with pleasure. "Lord it feels good to lie down." His silver-blue eyes glowed appreciatively as he gazed at her, surveying her body, visible through the thin cotton nightgown that was her only covering.

Reflexively driven by an instinct beyond control, his body responded. David laughed ruefully. "On second thought, maybe I'd better go."

"Don't you dare!" Pushing aside her apprehension about the wisdom of what she was doing, Julia slid into bed next to him and pulled the light cover over them both.

Nestled against him, she breathed in the heady, natural scent of him and worked hard at controlling her more basic urges. Softly, she said, "You need to rest or you won't be good for anything. Now just close your eyes and go to sleep."

He smiled tenderly, drawing her closer. "Yes, ma'am." Julia relaxed against him. Or at least she tried to. Sleep remained elusive.

David was too exhausted to have that problem. His eyelids slid inexorably downward, fluttered once as though he had to check to make sure she was really still there, then closed.

His breathing became deep and regular. The powerful arms holding her relaxed slightly, but did not let go. He sighed contentedly and, in his sleep, he smiled.

CHAPTER ELEVEN

Julia awoke to the touch of warm moist lips tugging gently at her nipples.

She groaned softly, not wanting to interrupt what seemed like a beautiful dream, only to realize with a start that the dream was reality. David loomed above her, his features shadowed in the early dawn light and his eyes glittering with need he could no longer suppress.

"I always prided myself on my self-control," he muttered thickly as he raised his head and gazed down at her. "But with you, it's shot to hell."

Pretense was beyond her. She smiled tenderly as she said simply, "I'm glad."

He hesitated a moment longer, his gaze holding hers as together they spoke what they could not yet put into words. Then the last of his tenuous restraint snapped and he lowered himself onto her.

Julia gasped. Before when they had made love, David had treated her like the most delicate crystal, liable to shatter in his hands. She had felt the latent power in him, but not the raw irresistible strength that could, should he choose, bend her helplessly to his will.

This time was different. He held back nothing as he made her vividly, shockingly aware of the full immensity of difference between them.

Where she was soft and pliant, he was all hard, driving demand. Where she yielded, he took. Where she attempted to retreat, he pursued.

His thigh did not probe gently between her legs as before but thrust urgently. Her muscles instinctively stiffened in rebellion, only to melt as he took the weight of her breast in his callused palm, his thumb rubbing back and forth across the hardened crest.

As she opened for him, he pressed his advantage further, dropping heated kisses down the smooth expanse of her abdomen to the nest of dampening curls below.

Julia cried out softly, her hips trying to arch against him but held immobile by his relentless strength. Frustration added a biting edge to her pleasure.

Only her hands could move, clasping his back, stroking the corded muscles lightly overlaid by rough silk skin. The heat radiating from him made her gasp. She might have been back in the desert, only now the danger was not death but the oblivion of dazzling pleasure.

Never had she been more vividly aware of herself as a woman or of what that meant to a man of David's power and virility.

She held within her the timeless rhythms of waters lapping against ancient shores. She could surround and engulf him, but never destroy. Without him to honor her power, what purpose did she have? Without her to nurture his seed, what reason for his life?

His burnished skin was stretched tautly over his high-boned cheeks and a jagged pulse beat in his throat. As his fingers found her and probed gently inward, Julia moaned helplessly.

Their eyes met, hers as softly violet as the sky at dawn, his crystalline steel torn from the pure blue sky, sent surging earthward to pierce the secret moss-draped cavern.

He waited through timeless moments, fine-tuning her body to respond to him alone, delaying the instant of release until she thought she would go mad for the waiting.

At last he lifted some measure of his weight from her, allowing her lower body to move. She cried out in relief only to have the sound die away into a groan of sheer delight as he grasped her hips and brought her against the hardened power of his manhood.

Not slowly, but with the relentless grace of a stag surging through a verdant glen, he plunged forward. She gasped in surprise mingled with the tiniest dart of fear. Stiffening with the expectation of pain, she found only shattering joy.

David had known, far better than she could, how ready she was for him. He filled her totally, driving out the hollow ache of emptiness and replacing it with burgeoning wonder.

The powerful muscles of his arms and chest rippled sinuously as he held himself above her, touching her nowhere but in the depths of her being. Gently he smoothed away tendrils of ebony hair clinging to her forehead and smiled reassuringly as he gave her time to become accustomed to his possession.

"David . . . I don't think I can bear this . . . !"

"You can . . . you will . . ." he grated. "God, you're so lovely . . . tight and hot . . . I can't have enough of you!"

"All of me . . . yours . . . I can't hold anything . . . back . . ."

"Don't try," he demanded, hard and potent and infinitely determined. "I won't stop until you're completely mine."

She wanted to tell him that she already was, but there was no chance for that. With deep, slow strokes he began to move inside her, igniting a fire storm of desire that drove out all sense of herself apart from him.

Her head tossed back and forth against the pillows, her skin glowing with a fine sheen of perspiration. Never could she have imagined the sensations David was unloosing in her. Every cell of her body and chamber of her soul were being invaded by radiant golden light.

Her breath became little more than gasping pants. The rush of blood in her ears drowned out all other sound, filling her with the torrent of her own life surging forth to meet his.

They crested together, riding a high, wide wave of sun-shattered water, climbing further and further into an azure sky. For a moment out of time they hung suspended, washed by flecks of foam and the dancing music of eternity.

The moment ended, the wave ebbed, and they arrived as exhausted survivors on a shore an infinity from where they had begun.

Aftershocks made them tremble as David fell onto his back and drew her to him. He did not speak. She guessed he was no more capable of that than herself. But one large, warm hand gently stroked her tumbled hair as the other caressed the smooth line of her back.

Gradually the tremors began to subside and their heartbeats returned to normal. Languidly content, Julia was close to sleep when David's deep, rumbling laughter drew her back to consciousness.

"What's funny?" she murmured uncertainly.

He gazed down at her, his eyes so tender that her lips parted in a silent exclamation of wonder. "I am," he said. "All my adult life I've taken pride in the fact that I can control myself, even under the worst circumstances. That got me through 'Nam, made me an astronaut, and brought me all the way to today. But one small, lovely woman makes a mockery of all my self-restraint."

Julia burrowed her head against his shoulder, unwilling to look at him again. His tone was ruefully humorous, but she wondered what he really thought. Did he resent her power over him?

How unfair if he did, since she was every bit as helpless to resist him. Their coming together had been a merging of equal wills and equal needs. No one was the victor, or the loser.

He felt her withdrawal and was puzzled by it. Moving slightly, he cupped the back of her head in his hand and urged her closer. "Julia . . . what's wrong . . . ?"

"Nothing," she insisted too quickly. "Only . . . it's not all on one side, you know. I feel the same way you do."

He was silent for a moment, absorbing that. She felt the brief flash of tension fade from him as though it had never been. "Sweetheart . . ." he murmured tenderly, "I know that. Your response was unmistakable." He smiled down at her so sweetly that her breath caught in her throat. "No man was ever so fortunate. You're perfect for me."

Absurdly, she felt like crying. Coming on top of the tormenting need and overwhelming ecstasy she had already experienced, his tender reassurance was almost too much.

She swallowed hastily and managed a watery smile. "I feel the same way about you."

"I'm glad," he said soberly. "It must be hell on earth when only half a couple feels like this."

A couple? Julia turned that over in her mind, savoring it. She had never been part of a twosome before. It gave her a nice feeling of security and purpose, as well as a driving need to know more, ideally everything, about the man who was truly the other half of herself.

"David . . . would you do me a favor?"

He cast her a wry look. "Don't tempt me. The spirit is more than willing but the flesh needs a little time to recuperate."

Despite her best efforts to prevent it, she blushed. "I didn't mean that!"

He chuckled, clearly enjoying her disconcertion. "No? What then?"

"Be serious. I just wanted to talk, that's all."

He made a show of sighing with relief. "I can manage that . . . I think. What do you want to talk about?"

"Ourselves . . . each other."

"Sounds good. There's so much I still don't know about you. For instance . . ."

"Wait a minute," Julia protested laughingly. "This was my idea. I should get to go first."

"Hmmm . . ." He pretended to think it over while he settled himself even more comfortably against her. "All right. What do you want to know?"

"Everything, but I'll start with something simple. Where were you born?"

"Chicago. I lived there until I was eighteen, when I joined the Army."

"What made you decide to do that?"

"They were still drafting people back then. Volunteering was supposed to be a good way of assuring a better assignment. Not that it worked for me. I went straight from boot camp to 'Nam."

Carefully, unsure of how far he would allow her to intrude on his private life, she asked, "Were you married by then?"

His chin rested against the top of her head as she felt him nod. "Yes, Cathleen and I decided not to wait. The ceremony took place just before I shipped out."

She was relieved when he didn't ask how she knew he had been married until she realized he might well presume she had some sort of dossier on him. Certainly he knew enough about how businesses like hers operated to make that assumption.

Her discomfort with what had seemed a perfectly sensible business decision came flooding back as she said quickly, "You don't have to tell me anything more. I really don't have the right to ask these questions, any more than I did to . . ."

David turned over suddenly, pressing her into the mattress with tender strength. His manhood, quiescent now but potent with remembered strength, brushed the sensitive skin of her upper thighs. "You do have the right, Julia. I gave it to you when we made love." His eyes met hers as he added, "I hope it works both ways."

She nodded, her eyes wide and guileless in their openness. "What do you want to know?"

He chuckled throatily. "As you said, everything. But to start with, if you weren't running Uncle Thaddeus's business, what would you be doing?"

That question brought her up short. She had taken too great pains to avoid thinking about just that point to confront it easily. "I don't know . . . besides, what does it matter? I do run the business."

"You say that as though it's as inevitable as the earth circling the sun," he murmured sardonically. "Didn't you ever hear of free will?"

"Are we going to have another discussion about responsibilities?" she asked. She didn't want to talk about the business. That might inevitably lead to a discussion of Skyward's financing and the decision she had to make soon.

But David refused to take the hint. "I don't believe for a moment that you're happy with what you're doing. You were forced into a position you would never have chosen for yourself. So how long do you think you can put up with it?"

Julia drew away from him. Suddenly she felt exposed and afraid. The sheet she pulled over herself offered only the illusion of protection. "You don't seem to have a very high opinion of me," she murmured.

His expression softened, becoming so tender that she looked away. But she could not block out his quiet words. "On the contrary. I think you're a beautiful, gentle woman whose family is taking advantage of your good nature. They've burdened you with responsibilities you shouldn't be carrying."

"You make it sound as though I'm some hothouse flower who can't survive in the big, cold world."

"You're deliberately misunderstanding me," he insisted patiently. "All I'm saying is that you should pick your own arena in which to prove yourself, not let others do it for you. I just can't believe you're cut out for this kind of work."

"And why not?" she demanded. Never mind that she had suspected the same thing herself.

"Because you're not tough enough. Look how worried you are about Skyward's success. You came here ready to pull out. That's not the mark of a true venture capitalist. Those guys have nerves of steel."

Julia didn't know whether to agree with him or get mad. On the one hand, she knew her nature was nothing at all like Uncle Thaddeus's. The very qualities of ruthlessness and toughness that had made him so successful had also prevented him from really getting to know her. She doubted he had ever questioned that she would do what was expected of her.

And neither had she, until recently. Sometime in the last six months she had come to the conclusion that if the firm was going to continue to prosper, she had to be realistic about her own strengths and weaknesses.

"I may not be as tough as the others," she admitted, "but I have a few other things going for me."

David nodded, touching a gentle hand to her

cheek. "More than anyone else I know. You have enormous sensitivity to other people, plus you're very intelligent and hardworking. But is that enough to succeed in your business?"

"I guess it has to be, because I'm not about to pretend to be something I'm not."

"You're too smart to just leave it like that," he said quietly. "My guess is you've thought this whole problem over pretty thoroughly. I'll bet I can even guess what you decided."

Julia wasn't sure she wanted him to continue, to put into words the essence of the barrier between them. But she sensed he was determined to get it out into the open.

Resignedly, she said, "It's no secret. I figured out the only way I can keep the firm prospering under my leadership is to back away from the riskier businesses and concentrate on those that may not bring in as much profit but have far less chance of failing."

"Like Skyward."

It wasn't a question and she was grateful for that, since she wouldn't have known how to answer him.

By every logical criteria, if the rocket launch failed, she should sever all financial ties with him no matter what the cost to their personal relationship.

Yet even as she tried to tell herself she would do what she had to do, Julia doubted it was that cut and dried. She was torn between burdensome professional responsibilities and the natural desire of a woman in love to give her man everything he needed.

In the aftermath of ecstasy, weariness overcame her. She was tired of fighting against herself, tired of worrying and wondering, tired of trying to guess what tomorrow would bring.

The new day had already arrived and soon she would have to deal not with tremulous fears but with inescapable reality.

CHAPTER TWELVE

It was very quiet in the communications trailer. The only sounds were the steady drone of machinery and the click of the digital clock counting down the last hour to launch.

So far everything had gone smoothly. Among the crew of scientists and technicians, Julia could sense a clear spirit of optimism. Yet David remained oddly apprehensive.

She told herself it was only because of everyone involved, he had the most to lose. He had, after all, poured his heart and soul into the project. Naturally he would be feeling the tension as the last moments ticked away.

But she couldn't shake the worry that something more than ordinary stress was at work. As he stubbornly went over the same checks again and again, always getting the same "go" results, even his loyal staff became perplexed.

Cal cast him a worried look, but said nothing. Like the others, she had come too far with him to question anything he did.

"Let's take another look at the fuel-line pressure," David said quietly. A low sigh rippled through the half-dozen people crammed into the small space, but no one argued. With the smoothness of practice, they began the check one more time.

It was very hot in the trailer. The air conditioner could not compensate for the heat of machinery and people in such close quarters. Julia pulled a handkerchief from the back pocket of her shorts and wiped her forehead.

Her ebony hair was swept up in a loose bun at the back of her head, but tendrils had already escaped to curl around the back of her neck. The shower she had taken that morning was barely a memory. Too many cups of coffee made her stomach burn.

The fuel line checked out perfectly, yet David remained dissatisfied. Another hold was called while voltage to the on-board computer was confirmed.

They were in the middle of that when Wilshire stuck his head in the trailer. "What's going on?" he demanded irately. "That's the second time the count has stopped."

"We're just being cautious," David told him, his tone dismissive. The vice-president refused to take the hint. He shoved his way into the already overcrowded space, ignoring the harassed looks of the crew members who had to squeeze out of his way.

"Don't give me that, Sherwood. If there's a problem, I want to know about it."

David's mouth tightened. His patience was badly

strained. The half-formed worries he could not shake were taking their toll. He rose slowly, his face taut and his eyes darkening to the shade of a storm-tossed sea as he surveyed the vice-president.

All those who knew him understood the signals. If they could have removed themselves from the scene, they would have. But they were trapped, the countdown was continuing, and it looked as though there was about to be an ignition that had nothing whatsoever to do with the rocket.

Until Julia smoothly insinuated herself between the two men. Taking Wilshire's arm, she smiled brightly. "It's terribly hot in here, isn't it? Let's go outside and I'll tell you all about what we've been doing."

He cast her a suspicious look before glancing back at David. What he saw decided him. As arrogant and dictatorial as he was, Wilshire wasn't foolish enough to confront a man clearly pushing up against the edge of his limits.

"All right," he agreed sullenly. "But you'd better level with me. I'm not going to be kept in the dark."

"Of course not," Julia murmured soothingly, beating down the urge to say something quite different. For two cents, she would have delivered a swift kick to the butt of the pompous intruder. But for David's sake, she would do her diplomatic best.

From the corner of her eye, she caught the wryly grateful glance he shot her. That gave her the encouragement she needed to gently but firmly steer Wilshire from the trailer.

Outside, the heat hit them like a blast from a smelting furnace. But at least there was a slight breeze and the shade of the awning. Wilshire grudgingly took his seat and accepted the cold can of beer she pulled from a nearby cooler.

He took a long swallow of it before he said, "I suppose you think I was out of line to go in there but, dammit, too much is riding on this to let some crazy astronaut blow it!"

"David isn't about to 'blow' it," Julia said quietly. Ignoring the apprehensive looks of his three assistants, she took a seat beside Wilshire and opened her own beer. It was early in the day to begin drinking, but under the circumstances she was going to forget that.

She took a sip, letting the crisp liquid soothe her parched throat, before she went on politely but firmly, "David is simply doing everything possible to make sure the launch goes well. You wouldn't want him to do less, would you?"

"No . . . but what's with these halts on the countdown?"

She smothered a sigh, wishing she had some simple answer for him. There was none. In the absence of any clear sign of trouble, such delays were inexplicable.

Carefully, she said, "David has enormous experience in this area. Apparently his instincts are telling him to go slowly."

"Instincts? You mean our multimillion-dollar satellite is riding on the gut feelings of a space jockey?" He glared at her, making no effort to hide his outrage.

"What's wrong with that?" she countered softly. "Don't you sometimes rely on your own intuition to make judgments?"

"If I did," Wilshire muttered, "I would never have wound up in this spot." He took another swallow of the beer and shook his head. "If you ask me, Sherwood's just getting cold feet. He knows it's time to put up or shut up, and he's running scared."

Julia bristled but managed to face him calmly. "You're underestimating him again. He doesn't scare."

"Oh, no?" Wilshire belched and pressed a hand to his stomach. Instantly an aide proffered a roll of stomach tablets. He took one without a word and popped it into his mouth, sucking hard for several moments.

At length he cocked his balding pate toward the rocket sitting off in the distance. "The hardest thing in the world is to put everything you've got on the line. Plenty of men will back off from that."

"Yes," Julia agreed softly, "that's true. But David has gone the last mile before. He knows what it is to risk everything and lose. Now he's ready to win."

Wilshire slumped down in his chair, his eyes still on

the rocket. Grimly, he said, "God help him if he's wrong. Nobody will ever trust him again."

She resisted the temptation to point out that no matter what happened with the rocket, David would always have her trust. Wilshire's words had set off an uncomfortable train of thought.

Was David's profound apprehension related strictly to his professional instincts, or was his personal predicament getting in the way? Their lovemaking the night before had been glorious, but it might also have further complicated an already difficult situation.

It was bad enough to have both financial security and the fulfillment of a dream riding on the outcome of the launch. Throw in the fact that he might believe failure would mean losing her and it was easy to see why he was tied up in knots.

Julia silently berated herself for not having been more candid with him. Only her own insecurities had prevented her from talking openly about the decision she had to make and assuring him she wanted a future together no matter what.

Yet would any such assurances have worked? David was an intensely proud man. If he couldn't offer her a secure, productive life, he might have concluded it was better to offer nothing at all.

Biting her lip, she glanced at the closed door of the trailer. If only she could go in there and tell him what was in her heart. But with so many other people present, and time ticking inexorably away, that was impossible.

She could only wait as the countdown continued and the great rocket prepared to rumble into life.

Ten minutes from launch, David called another halt. It lasted just long enough to check the on-board computer yet again. With the count resumed, Julia and Wilshire were both on the edge of their seats. David's voice reached them over the microphone that broadcast what was going on in the control trailer to those who couldn't fit inside.

Two minutes from ignition, the gantry was rolled aside. Ninety seconds later the final firing sequence began. It was proceeding smoothly with ignition expected at five seconds before lift-off.

David's voice was steady as he ticked off the numbers, "Ten . . . nine . . . eight . . . seven . . . six . . . five . . . four . . ."

Without realizing that she did so, Julia was on her feet. Her stomach clenched painfully as she stared out at the unchanged vista.

Where was the plume of smoke heralding successful firing of the engines? Where was the tongue of yellow flame that would lift the rocket heavenward?

Instead there was only the silence of the desert and the thudding of her own heart. Until David's voice suddenly grated over the microphone, "Shut down all systems. Emergency abort."

Wilshire jumped up, his face red and his breathing

heavy. *"What's going on? What the hell is happening?"*

Julia didn't bother to answer him. She was heading toward the trailer when the door flew open and David emerged with Cal and several of the other scientists on his heels.

As they ran for the nearest jeeps, Julia followed doggedly. She jumped in beside him before he could object and held on for dear life as the vehicle careened along the rutted road leading to the gantry.

Screeching to a halt, David jumped out and grabbed a bag of tools from the back as he turned to the crew. "Everybody stay here until I find out what's wrong."

"You can't go in there alone, Davey," Cal objected, her weathered face creased with worry.

"I'm not putting anyone else at risk," he insisted stubbornly. "Don't move until I give the 'all clear.' "

Julia's eyes met his for an instant: his grimly determined, hers filled with questions and dawning fear. She took a step forward, mutely lifting a hand to try to hold him.

With a visible effort, he wrenched his gaze from her and turned away, racing toward the rocket.

Instinctively, Julia tried to go after him, only to be stopped by Cal and another scientist, gripping her arms. "Let him be, honey," Cal murmured gently. "He's got to do what he's got to do."

Perhaps, but that didn't make it any easier for her to stand by and watch him vanish into the small room

158

at the base of the gantry that gave access to the inner workings of the massive rocket.

Around her, the half-dozen men who had come with them stood tensely, their hands jammed in their pockets and their shoulders hunched against some unseen psychic wind that threatened to upset them all.

Cal's hand remained on her arm, but Julia barely noticed it. Her attention was focused on the small room at the base of the gantry, into which David had vanished.

The sense of time passing ground to a halt. The unblinking eye of the sun gazed down at the desert, stretching endlessly to all horizons. Around the great stone buttes streaked with vermilion and gold the air circled and danced, murmuring in voices no man could understand.

Around the rocket the wind was mournful, full of expectation and dread.

Julia shivered. She moved slightly away from Cal and wrapped her arms around herself. A leaden sense of coldness was growing in her, blocking out the heat.

Beneath the glowing sun, brushed by arid wind, she felt the icy hand of death.

"David . . ." Even as his name left her, joining the singing wind, she was moving forward. Evading Cal's hand and ignoring the scientists' shouts, she ran toward the gantry. Her heart beat painfully and her breathing was labored. She seemed to be moving in

slow motion, toward some distant goal slipping beyond her grasp.

The explosion registered on her eyes first, then on her brain. She opened her mouth to scream, only to be stopped by the rushing wall of pressure that lifted her slender body and tossed her like a rag doll into the air.

The world turned upside down, spun sickeningly, then righted itself too abruptly as she landed hard on her back, her head striking the ground with an agonizing crack.

She lay, unblinking, gazing up at the sun. There was no pain, only a reassuring sense of peace that banished all fear.

She could hear David, saying her name as he had at the height of their lovemaking, and wanted to go to him. But when she tried to move, she could not. Frustration banished the peace.

The air turned sharply crystalline, hurting her eyes. The sand seemed to undulate beneath her. She was alone and frightened, not understanding what was happening. She heard David again, farther away, and tried to call to him, but no sound emerged.

There was only the desert wind lit by a crimson tear falling from the sun into darkness.

CHAPTER THIRTEEN

All things considered, she got off lightly. Coming to within minutes after losing consciousness, she found Cal bending over her, holding a cloth to her injured head and barking instructions to the men.

"Radio the base and tell them we're bringing in casualties. Joe, you and Fred get the fire extinguishers from the jeeps and get to work on that fire."

As Julia shifted slightly, Cal's attention returned to her. "And you just stay where you are, young lady! The idea of running off like that . . . ! Don't you have any more sense?"

"I . . . guess not. . . . Where's David?"

"We don't know yet. Phil and Charlie got inside the gantry. They'll report any minute."

"You said . . . fire . . ."

"Not in the gantry," Cal explained quickly, correctly reading her terror. "It's the rocket. Part of it blew. We don't know how much yet."

Unable to stay still, Julia stubbornly struggled upward. She was relieved that her body obeyed, more or less. She needed to lean on Cal, but at least the terrifying instant of paralysis was over.

"Help me up . . . please . . ."

"I don't think you should stand yet, honey. You're liable to be worse off than you realize."

Julia shook her head dazedly, ignoring the waves of pain that washed over her. "No . . . I have to find David . . ."

"I told you, Phil and Charlie will bring him out. You've got to take it easy . . ." Cal broke off, feeling the sudden tension that raced through Julia. She turned, her weathered face tightening as she saw the still form being carried from the gantry room.

Without another word, she helped Julia to her feet and kept her upright as the grim-faced men approached. "Can't tell how bad it is yet," Charlie said as he passed them. "Got to get him back to base fast."

Julia swayed helplessly, her eyes on David. Beneath his tan, his skin was ashen. A long, ugly gash stretched from below his hairline down the left side of his brow to his cheek.

It was still bleeding, though not as badly as the wounds to his arms and legs. Metal fragments had struck him all over, some threatening vital veins and arteries. Yet miraculously he was not hemorrhaging, at least so far as she could see.

Without thought for her own condition, Julia limped hurriedly to the jeep. There was just room for her to crouch in the back beside David's unmoving form. Cal jumped into the front seat and a gray-bearded scientist slid behind the wheel.

As he turned the ignition and jammed the accelerator to the floor, he cast Julia an anxious glance. "Hold on, Ms. Cabot. We're in for a hell of a ride."

That was an understatement. At some time in his life Charlie must have nurtured dreams of becoming a Formula 500 racer. He took the sharpest curves on two wheels and in the straightaways seemed barely to touch the ground.

Julia clung to the back of her seat with one hand and used the other to steady David. She did not take her eyes from him even as they roared into Arroyo.

The jeep screeched to a halt in front of the cabin. Charlie jumped out and, assisted by other crew members, carried David inside. He returned swiftly for Julia, only to find her making her own way through the door.

"What's being done for him?" she demanded without preamble.

Charlie gestured toward the bedroom. "Cal's a paramedic. She'll take good care of him until we can get more help." Gently, he added, "In the meantime, you've got to sit down and rest."

"I'm fine," Julia insisted. Never mind the dull throb of her head or the growing suspicion that several of her ribs weren't quite right. "I'll stay out of the way, but I need to see David."

Charlie didn't try to stop her. Gray-bearded he might be, but he wasn't so old that he couldn't recognize what had been happening between his boss and their visitor. With a sigh, he stepped aside and held the bedroom door open for her.

Julia entered hesitantly, determined to keep control of herself no matter what. Her throat was clenched and she barely breathed as she gazed at the bed.

David lay just as he had been put down by the men, his arms and legs stretched out and his whole body looking vividly defenseless. He was still deeply unconscious. His breathing was slow and labored, and his color remained gray.

Cal had wasted no time getting to work. She swiftly attached a blood-pressure cuff, took a reading, and then carefully lifted each of David's eyelids to shine a pinpoint of light on his pupils.

As she glanced up and saw Julia standing white-faced and shaking by the door, she said quietly, "His pressure is low, but not dangerously so. Both pupils are equally dilated, which suggests there may not be serious head injuries."

"Any sign of internal bleeding?" Julia forced herself to ask.

"Not so far. But we'd better get him moved to a hospital as quickly as possible."

That turned out to be more difficult than anyone had expected. As Julia sank down beside the bed, taking David's hand in her own, Charlie went to inquire about a helicopter ambulance. He came back with bad news.

"They've had a major pileup on the highway about twenty miles from here. All their mobile facilities are in use, and there's no chance of getting them free for at least a couple of hours. Worse yet, the weather is closing in. We look to have a major dust storm soon, which would keep them from getting to us at all."

"So what do they suggest we do?" Cal demanded.

"Get him stabilized and keep an eye on him. We can try another hospital, but considering how remote we are, the chances of anyone arriving sooner are pretty dim."

Weak and in pain though she was, Julia insisted on helping Cal. Together they stripped off David's clothes and tended to the multitude of shrapnel wounds covering his body.

Wiping the dried blood from his legs, she had to swallow hard to keep from crying. By some miracle, none of the cuts was really severe. Only a few looked bad enough to even leave scars. But several were within millimeters of veins and arteries. Getting a tight grip on herself, she refused to think of how close he had come to death.

When David seemed to be resting more comfortably, she finally agreed to let Cal check her over. Aside from an impressive bump on the back of her head and the ribs that turned out to be bruised rather than broken, she was in good shape.

"You used up a big piece of luck back there," Cal said. "Be glad it was there when you needed it and don't try to press it further."

Wearily, Julia agreed. With the knowledge that David would survive, the last of her energy was fading fast. It was all she could do to sink down on the bed beside him and let Cal cover them both up before she drifted away into healing sleep.

She woke some hours later with the sound of the explosion echoing in her dreams. Disoriented, she sat up quickly and looked around, only to fall back against the pillows when she found David beside her.

He was sleeping deeply, the gray tinge gone from his face and his breathing normal. Reaching out a hand, she touched him carefully, barely brushing her fingertips against his shoulder.

His skin was warm, but not unnaturally so. Beneath her gentle touch, she could feel the solid strength of him undiminished by his ordeal.

Reassured, Julia slid from the bed. As she stood, her head reeled dizzily. She had to keep a hand on the wall to steady herself as she made her way to the bathroom.

Staring into the mirror above the sink, she gasped softly. Perhaps it was just as well that David wasn't conscious; she wouldn't have wanted him to see her like this.

Her hair was a tangled mess dulled by sand and dust. Her face was streaked by grime, as was all the rest of her. The shirt and shorts she wore were filthy and tattered.

Resolutely stripping them off, she stepped into the

shower. The cool water cleared her head enough to banish the dizziness. She was able to wash most of herself, except for the colorful bruises along her ribs and the scrapes along her arms and legs.

Wrapped in a towel, she padded back to the bedroom to check on David again and get clean clothes. Her eyes did not leave him as she hurriedly dressed and dried her hair.

Convinced that he was resting comfortably, she left the cabin in search of Cal. A glance at the sky confirmed that the prediction of bad weather had been correct. The azure expanse was eclipsed by a thick, yellowish haze that hinted at far worse to come. Already the rocket, barely a mile away, was all but invisible.

With the dust storm closing in, the scientists had gathered in the mess hall to share their worries and try to come up with solutions. They weren't being helped by an irate Wilshire.

"I don't give a damn what any of you say," he snapped. "This whole thing's a disaster and VICOM is pulling out."

"If you'll just give us a chance," Cal said quietly, "we already know what went wrong and it's not that difficult to correct."

"I'm not interested in that. I want the satellite removed and crated for shipment back to our labs immediately."

"No!" Julia could not hold back her angry refusal.

The surprised scientists cleared a path for her as she hurried to Cal's side.

"Honey, you shouldn't be out of bed. Is something wrong with David?"

"He's resting comfortably and I'm fine, or at least I was until I came in here and heard this nonsense." Confronting Wilshire, she said flatly, "Do I really have to remind you that under the terms of your agreement with Skyward, we have a second launch opportunity one week from now?"

The vice-president scowled. "That's technically correct but under the circumstances there is no reason to . . ."

Julia cut him off with an impatient gesture and turned to Cal. "You said you knew what had gone wrong and how to fix it."

"That's right. A microprocessor in the computer that relays information to the booster rocket failed. Pilgrim's internal security systems automatically picked up on that and, to protect itself, it shut down."

"So no damage was done to the rocket itself or the satellite?"

Cal shook her head. "David severed the wiring leading from the booster fuel tanks to the main ones. So the explosion was confined."

"None of which means you're going to be able to get that thing off the ground," Wilshire broke in vehemently.

"Why not?" Julia asked. She couldn't pretend to understand all the intricacies of what had happened,

168

but it did seem to be far less serious than it might have been. No one had to tell her that was because David had risked his life to save Pilgrim.

Cal hesitated. She glanced from Julia to the other scientists, who shifted uneasily. Finally, she said, "Mr. Wilshire is alluding to the fact that in order to launch we would have to replace the entire booster rocket, including its on-board control computer. The equipment is available, but it's extremely expensive."

Julia took a deep breath, steeling herself for what she feared was coming. Quietly, she asked, "How expensive?"

"A million . . . maybe slightly more."

She blanched. Under the best circumstances, she thought long and hard before spending that kind of money. But coming on top of the vast sums already invested in Skyward . . .

"I told you," Wilshire gloated. "Only an idiot would throw good money after bad."

His self-satisfied smirk riled Julia. Yet she knew that his was the attitude any of her colleagues would take. *Cut your losses and run.* She could almost hear Uncle Thaddeus saying that and knew with a sinking heart that her family and the other shareholders in Cabot Venture Financing would feel the same way.

How could she betray their interests? Yet how could she stand by and let David's dream be destroyed?

"I have to do some thinking about this," she said finally. "Just sit tight for a while."

"There's no reason for that!" Wilshire protested. "I want that satellite removed now!"

Julia ignored him. Quietly, with the innate authority so much a part of her that she wasn't even aware of it, she gave her instructions. "With this storm closing in, it will be a while before we can get back out to the rocket. But we can make good use of the time here at base. Cal, I'd like you to get me confirmation that the booster rocket can be delivered and installed in time for the next launch date. While that's being done, I'd appreciate it if the rest of you would completely check out the communications setup and make sure there's no problem with the rest of the control systems."

She glanced around, mildly surprised by their respectful nods. "Have I forgotten anything?"

"Doesn't appear so, honey," Cal chuckled. "You heard the lady, fellows. Let's get to work."

The scientists hurried off and Wilshire left grumbling. Julia watched them all go with relief. When the door closed on the last one, she slumped slightly. The decision she had to make almost overwhelmed her, yet she was determined to do what was right for all concerned.

Her hands shook as she poured herself a cup of coffee and took a seat at one of the long wooden tables. Staring off into space, she began to do some very serious calculations.

Half an hour later Cal came in to confirm that the rocket booster could be delivered in time. "It'll be tight, but if we work around the clock, we can get it installed before the next launch window opens."

"When do they need authorization to ship?"

"To meet our schedule, you have to commit to the purchase no later than the end of today."

Perhaps that was just as well. She didn't want a lot of time to chew over her problem. "All right, I'll decide before then. Right now, I want to check on David."

"Be careful out there," Cal called to her as she left the mess tent. "This storm's a humdinger."

That it was. Julia had to fight her way across the compound, battling powerful gusts of wind that whipped sand into her face and eyes. She stumbled into the cabin and slammed the door behind her, pausing a moment to catch her breath.

A sound from the bedroom drew her up short. Forgetting herself, she hurried in there just in time to find David trying to stand up. He staggered and would have fallen if she hadn't reached him in time.

"What are you doing? You'll hurt yourself!"

"I already hurt," he muttered between tightly clenched teeth. Weak as he was, he could not resist as she lowered him back onto the bed. His fists clenched in frustration as he demanded, "What the hell happened?"

"There was an explosion in the rocket booster."

David shut his eyes for a moment. When he opened them again, she could see the hard glitter of despair. His voice was expressionless as he said, "I thought so. We were supposed to be feeding fuel only to the ignition system of the main rocket, but it reached the booster instead."

Unable to bear the bleakness of his gaze, Julia said, "The damage was limited because of . . . what you did. Only the booster needs to be replaced."

He laughed humorlessly. *"Only?"* You might as well say we only need to start from scratch. Do you have any idea what those things cost?"

It was clear he didn't think she had the slightest idea. Matter-of-factly, she said, "About a million dollars."

David's surprise was gratifying, if only briefly. His mouth tightened as he demanded, "Who told you that?"

"Cal. She's also confirmed that a new booster can be delivered in time to make the next launch window." Taking a deep breath, Julia sat down beside him on the bed, met his angry gaze unflinchingly, and said, "I've figured out how to pay for it."

He stared at her silently, his expression unfathomable. His lack of response made her wonder if he had understood. Softly, she said, "David, I'm telling you you'll have the money."

A moment longer he looked at her, taking in her tremulous smile and the softness of her eyes. She was so damn lovely, and so vulnerable.

His throat tightened as he recognized both the full magnitude of what she was offering him and its source. She loved him, and in her love was making a decision that would cost far more than money.

His hand tightened on hers as he glanced away. Fixing his eyes on the wall, he said, "I can't take it, Julia. Skyward is finished."

CHAPTER FOURTEEN

"Finished . . . ?" Julia shook her head numbly. Surely she had heard him wrong. "I don't understand."

"There's nothing complicated about it. We're out of money so we're closing shop."

"But I just told you, you can have the money!"

"No!" He forced himself to sit up, grimacing with the pain but offering no concessions to it. Or her. "I won't take it. You've got too much at risk already."

"And if you stop now, I'll lose it all." She could make no sense of his reasoning. Why, after struggling so hard for so long, would he suddenly want to give up?

"You'll lose the money Cabot invested so far, but at least it wasn't your decision to come in on this and no one can blame you for it. You can get out now and start fresh."

"Thanks a lot! I just don't happen to want to do that."

"You don't have any choice."

That flat assertion robbed Julia of breath. She stared at him dazedly, willing him to say something, anything that would make it all right again.

His mouth was set in a hard, uncompromising line and his eyes were shuttered. He refused to look at her as he said, "I've done you enough damage. Don't expect me to compound it."

"You haven't . . . ! How can you take this attitude? Don't you realize that I lo . . ."

"You've said enough! Can't you take a hint? I want you to leave."

The force of the explosion that had knocked her around like a rag doll did not equal the impact of his words. Julia turned ashen. Her slender body shook and her eyes turned dark with pain. "You don't mean that . . ."

"For God's sake, what does it take to convince you! It's over. Go back to Boston and put your life back together. Forget about me."

Unspoken between them was the assertion that he intended to do the same. Before her very eyes, he was turning into a stranger. Someone hard and cold and unfeeling who seemed to have only disdain for her.

Julia rose stiffly. She was screaming inside, but pride refused to let her give voice to her anguish. Forget about him? The very idea was absurd. She would bear his mark for the rest of her life. But she didn't have to let him know that.

Coldly, she said, "You're forgetting something

yourself. Under the terms of your agreement with Cabot Venture Financing, I have final say on all major decisions likely to affect the survival of the business. You gave that up when you took our money."

David looked at her narrowly. "Just what are you saying?"

"That I don't choose to let Skyward fold without one more effort to save it. With or without your approval, the new rocket booster will be installed and a second launch attempted."

At last she had succeeded in genuinely puzzling him. "Why are you doing this?" he asked in bewilderment.

"I told you. Cabot has too much invested in Skyward to let it go under without a fight." Giving some slight release to her rage and hurt, she added, "You may be ready to give up, but I'm not!"

The barb struck home. David flinched and shot back, "You can't do this. I'm still in charge here and I say it's no go."

"Tough! I'm overriding you." Ignoring his futile efforts to pull himself from the bed, she turned her back and headed for the door. Her hand was on the knob when she glanced over her shoulder frostily. "You're out of commission. From now on, I'm giving the orders."

He fell back against the pillows with a groan and glared at her. "Like hell you will! Just wait until I get out of here . . ."

"Don't hold your breath. You've got more holes in

you than a sieve. By the time you're on your feet, Pilgrim will either have put that damn satellite in orbit or blown up in the attempt!"

With that she marched from the room, slamming the door behind her and closing her ears to the steady stream of curses emanating from the man who had made it clear he had no further use for her.

David might not, but the rest of the scientists felt differently. After making the necessary phone calls to transfer funds for the booster and assure its delivery, Julia called everyone together in the mess hall. The dust storm was still raging outside as she spelled out the situation to them.

"In the absence of . . . the usual leadership . . . I am exercising my right to assume control of this operation. It is my intention to restore Pilgrim to launch condition and meet our deadline with VICOM. If any of you has a problem going along with that, I want to know now."

Several of the men cleared their throats nervously, but most seemed relieved by her determination. They were undoubtedly loyal to David, but the project itself came first. Whatever had to be done to launch Pilgrim, they would give their best efforts.

"Did you . . . uh . . . tell David what you're planning?" Cal asked at length.

"Yes, and he disagrees. He wants to close Skyward down now."

At the shocked looks from the scientists, she said more gently, "You have to remember that he was injured today. He's not completely himself and his judgment can't be relied on. So I'm taking the decision out of his hands. We go for the second launch."

Not for a moment did she believe that David's thought processes were in any way impaired. He had been adamant in stating what he wanted. But it was kinder to let the scientists believe he had not really turned his back on them.

Throughout the remainder of that day and into the night, as the storm raged all around them, they worked to devise a precise plan for removing the damaged booster and replacing it, as well as a schedule for getting it all done in time.

"Like I said," Cal muttered when the weary group finally went off for a few hours rest, "it's going to be tight, but we'll make it."

Julia nodded tiredly. Since coming to Arroyo, she had encountered more stress and fatigue than she had ever experienced before. But not even that had prepared her for the leaden exhaustion she felt now. She had to sleep, and soon, or she would be no good to anyone.

"Cal . . . could I bunk with you?"

The older woman looked surprised for a moment, before understanding and sympathy softened her eyes. "Sure thing, honey. But I got to warn you, I snore."

Julia managed a weak laugh. As she and Cal made their way across the compound, she stalwartly kept her eyes away from David's cabin. Had she looked in that direction, she would have seen the bedroom light still burning and the silhouette of a man sitting up in bed with his head buried in his hands.

Four days later the new booster was maneuvered into place beside the rocket and the crew went to work securing it. In the intervening time, the rubble from the explosion had been completely cleared away and all systems pronounced operational.

Against the advice of both Cal and the doctor who had finally reached the base, David had emerged from his cabin to supervise the operation.

He said nothing to Julia, nor did she attempt to talk to him. They both took refuge in the vast amount of work that needed to be accomplished and kept their distance from each other.

Wilshire was a constant problem, forever getting under foot and complaining about anything and everything. Julia took it upon herself to keep him out of the scientists' way. She was immune to his constant carping. Nothing could possibly make her feel any worse than she already did.

Work proceeded around the clock to ready the rocket for the second attempt at a launch. The burden fell most heavily on David, who had to be present almost constantly.

Julia silently worried about him, fearing that he was pressing himself too hard too fast. But she said nothing. Instead she contented herself in seeing that he was kept as free of unnecessary worries as possible.

When the temperamental cook rebelled against the long hours and abruptly quit, she stepped into the breach, surprising herself with a skill she hadn't known she possessed. Everyone was too preoccupied to realize who was providing the warm, nourishing food available around the clock. But she was satisfied that every scrap got eaten.

When a couple of the jeeps broke down, restricting the team's ability to get back and forth between the rocket and base, she drove out to the gas station she had stopped at a lifetime ago and convinced the grizzly old mechanic to come out and repair them.

He stayed to watch in fascination as the final preparations for the second launch attempt got under way.

They were coming down to the wire, with no margin for error, but Julia told herself that this time there would be no mistakes. She said the same to Wilshire, who snorted in disbelief.

"The best I'm hoping for is that the satellite doesn't get blown up. If it's damaged, VICOM will sue not just Skyward but everyone else involved in this fiasco."

She sighed inwardly, but did not let him see her irritation. They were sitting under the canopy once again, waiting through the final minutes of the countdown.

So far there had been only one hold, for some minor problem that was quickly solved. At launch minus ten minutes, everything was going well.

The day was crystal clear with only a slight wind. Off in the distance, the rocket rose majestically. The satellite was in place, the boosters ready; everything that could possibly ensure success had been done.

All that remained was to wait while the final minutes ticked away.

At launch minus two, Julia stood up. She was nervous, but not as much as last time.

Then so much had ridden on the launch—all her hopes for the future. Now she only wanted to see it over and done with so that she could withdraw to lick her wounds.

The gantry was rolled away and the countdown proceeded. Over the loudspeaker, she could hear David beginning the firing sequence.

His voice was rock steady, but she thought she sensed an underlying tone of sadness she attributed to exhaustion.

"Ten . . . nine . . . eight . . . seven . . . six . . . five . . ."

A plume of white smoke appeared at the base of the rocket.

". . . four . . . three . . ."

A column of yellow flame roared to life.

". . . two . . . one . . . lift-off . . ."

As though in eerie obedience to that quietly uttered command, Pilgrim began to rise, first with aching slowness, then more swiftly.

The wave of explosive sound engulfed them. The ground trembled. The azure sky was cleaved in two by the pillar of smoke and fire lifting higher and higher into heaven with the rocket poised on top of it, shimmering in the sunlight.

Far out above the desert, it arched into its predetermined trajectory, taking it downrange into the orbit where the satellite would be deployed.

Julia watched as long as she could see anything, her eyes straining and her neck cramped. She was only dimly aware of Wilshire beside her, shaking his head dazedly.

When she glanced at him, he stared back defiantly. "It's not over yet. They've still got to launch the bird right."

Thirty minutes later, they did. Jettisoned by the booster rockets that functioned perfectly, the satellite entered geostationary orbit exactly on schedule. Its antennas deployed precisely as planned and within seconds its first signals were beaming earthward.

The cheer that went up from the Skyward team rivaled the roar of the rocket they had just launched. Their elation was wholehearted.

Not only had they accomplished what they had set out to do, but in doing so they had opened an entire new chapter in space exploration.

Julia found some small comfort in their happiness,

but nothing could really penetrate the wall of sadness surrounding her.

While the celebration was just beginning, she slipped away to David's cabin to collect her belongings and prepare to leave.

CHAPTER FIFTEEN

It was very quiet in the cabin. She could hear the joyful sounds of the exultant team outside, but inside there was only silence.

Her intention of packing quickly dissolved as she stared around the room where she had found such joy, and such pain.

Sparsely furnished and almost depressingly bare, it nonetheless had once been paradise to her. Now it was only a place she had to get away from quickly.

Finding her clothes in the closet, she folded them neatly and slipped them into her briefcase. Later she could think about changing out of her shorts and shirt, but just then she felt no urge to do so.

The elegantly tailored dress and impractical shoes were a remnant of another life. One that she somehow had to get back to.

The few toiletries she had left in the bathroom fit easily into her handbag. With that done, there was nothing more to keep her.

Yet she paused for a last look around, even though she knew she was only tormenting herself.

As her eyes misted with tears, a sob broke from her. Quickly she bit her lip. She would not, could not, give in to her grief. Not until she was far enough away to do so in private.

But it seemed that was not to be the case. Even as she felt a moment's relief that no one had been there to witness her despair, a sound from the door alerted her to the fact that she was not alone.

A bolt of shock shot through her as she turned to find David watching her.

He looked very tired and very tense, yet he was still the most devastatingly attractive man she had ever seen. Even as she tried to deny the effect he had on her, her heartbeat accelerated and a warm flush colored her cheeks.

Uncoiling his length from beside the door, he walked toward her, his eyes holding hers. She had to resist the impulse to step back. They were only a few feet apart when he asked softly, "What are you doing?"

"P-packing . . . my things . . ." Her voice sounded oddly breathless even to her own ears, almost as though she had run a great distance.

His bronzed legs, bare beneath his shorts, were planted slightly apart. His big hands hung loosely at his sides, the fingers coiling inward. "Why?"

Julia swallowed tightly, willing herself to stay calm. She tried to take a step toward the door, only to find she was rooted in place by the sheer force of his gaze.

"Because . . ." she managed at length, "it's time for me to leave."

Something hard and dangerous glittered in his crystalline blue eyes. As though of its own volition, his hand reached out to lightly touch her cheek.

At the brush of his callused fingers against her, Julia flinched. She was so painfully susceptible and terrifyingly vulnerable. If he guessed how easily he could make her forget everything, even her pride, she would be lost.

David dropped his hand but did not move back. Softly he said, "VICOM will be paying us for the launch within a couple of days. Once the funds have cleared, I'll buy back your interest in Skyward plus the considerable profit you've earned."

It was Julia's turn to be surprised. What he was offering would put millions in Cabot's pockets, but only at the cost of draining all his cash reserves.

"That doesn't make any sense," she protested. "You're not obligated to buy us out."

"I know. But you must realize that this will continue to be a very risky business for some time to come. It's better for you to get out of it. I'm just glad you'll be able to do it with a profit instead of a loss."

"Better . . . because I'm not tough enough?"

David sighed and ran a weary hand through his tousled hair. The well-remembered gesture reminded Julia sharply of the intimacy they had shared. All her resolution about not letting him get to her again was fading fast.

"That was a poor choice of words," he admitted gently. "You're about the strongest person I know. The problem is me. I just can't take the idea of your risking your professional success to support my business."

Her eyes widened slightly at this admission. Did he really see her that way? "I thought . . . that is, you seemed to have developed a very low opinion of me."

His mouth curved upward in a self-deprecating grin. "I was grasping at straws, using anything I could think of to get you to leave before you put even more at risk than you already had. When you refused to go, it seemed like a nightmare to me. I couldn't live with the idea of failing and making you look bad to all of Cabot's investors."

"I wouldn't have looked bad to them," Julia corrected quietly. "As you pointed out, the original decision to support you was Uncle Thaddeus's."

"But you put in the extra million for the booster."

She shrugged, as though stating what seemed obvious to her. "That wasn't Cabot money. I used my own."

"Your own?"

"That's right. Both sets of my grandparents left large trust funds for me. I guess I never had much use for them before, so they accumulated quite a bit of money. Once I remembered that, I knew how I could protect Skyward without betraying any of my professional responsibilities."

"How . . . how much was in these funds?"

She didn't want to answer that, but the hard set of his mouth warned her he wouldn't tolerate evasion. Reluctantly, she said, "A million, almost exactly."

"So you used every penny of your own money to buy that booster?"

Julia looked away uncomfortably. She knew he wouldn't believe for a moment that an emotionally uninvolved woman could take such an action. "It . . . seemed like a good idea at the time." Grasping her briefcase and handbag more firmly, she headed toward the door. "I've got to be going now. The flight to Boston is in a couple of hours."

"I see. . . . What about the buy-out?"

She stopped, blinking hard. Of course, he still wanted to sever his connection with Cabot. "Why don't you wait a few months? I don't imagine you'll be lacking for business now and you'll soon be able to recover sole ownership without draining your cash reserves. Naturally, in the meantime, I won't be interfering in any way."

He raised an eyebrow skeptically. "Oh, no? Then how come you already are?"

"What do you mean?"

"If you leave now, you'll just be forcing me to follow you to Boston."

The heated tenderness of his gaze settled over her, robbing her of strength. The briefcase and handbag suddenly seemed too heavy. Her arms trembled with the strain of holding them.

David moved slightly in front of her, his big, hard body blocking her path to the door. "Why don't you put those things down?" he suggested gently. "They're not going anywhere."

"I-I have a plane to catch . . ."

"We'll both catch it, in a few days." Her puzzled look made his smile deepen. Caressingly, he said, "I presume that after we're married, you'll want to visit your family."

Julia put down her burdens. More correctly, they dropped beside her feet. She took a deep breath and looked him straight in the eye. "If we're getting married, I want a few things straightened out first."

The sudden release of tension from him did not escape her. Confidently, she said, "For starters, please explain why you were so horrible to me."

"I'm sorry," he said huskily. "When the first launch failed, I felt as though I had lost everything. But not because of Skyward. After years of devoting my life to this, suddenly it didn't mean anywhere near as much as the fact that I had let you down."

"I didn't see it that way," she said briskly, fighting the urge to go to him. Realistically, she knew she couldn't hold out much longer, but once she was in his arms, everything else would be forgotten. "How could you let me walk out of your life?"

"I wasn't planning to. My intention was to do my damnedest to get my life back in shape as quickly as possible, so that I'd have something decent to offer you, then follow you to Boston and make such a pest of myself that you'd have to agree to marry me."

Dawning comprehension, and joy, sent rays of gold flitting through her violet eyes. "Oh . . . but instead I insisted on hanging around."

He nodded lovingly. "You're the most stubborn woman I've ever met."

"You're no slouch in that department yourself." She was smiling as she said that, the joy beginning to spill out of her.

With unaccustomed humility, he asked, "Do you think you might consider marrying me?"

"Didn't you just tell me I was going to?"

"Yes, but it occurred to me you might prefer to be asked."

"That's sensible. What will we do about Cabot? I can't run it from here."

"Do you want to run it?"

Julia didn't even have to think about that one. She shook her head firmly. "No, you were right about that all along. I've only been doing it because I thought I had no option, and also in a sense because I had to prove myself. But I've done that now and there's nothing to stop me from hiring someone to take over."

"What will your family think of that?"

She shrugged, moving toward him. "They won't like it, but they'll adjust. Anyway, you're my family now."

He groaned as his arms reached out to her, engulfing her in his gently fierce embrace. "And you're mine. Forever."

Long moments later, after they had shared a kiss that set both their hearts to racing and made the nearby bed beckon invitingly, Julia murmured, "Of course, I'll need to do something."

"You'll manage Skyward," David said promptly. "The one thing we've lacked all along is someone with good business sense who can cope with the clients and keep everything running smoothly. You've more than proved you can do that."

Pleased by so simple and satisfying a solution, she let the last of her concerns evaporate. The touch of David's mouth, warm and seeking, along the sensitive column of her throat was swiftly making all thought impossible.

But in the final moments before she yielded to the exquisite maelstrom of passion, she reflected on the mysteriousness of fate that had brought her to the desert to confront first death, then herself, and finally the man with whom she would share the future.

A future heralded by the empty gantry standing waiting in the sun and the promise of Pilgrim that dreams were all the more glorious when they became reality.

Author's Note

While all the characters and events of this story are the products of my imagination, they do have some basis in reality. In September 1982, Matagorda Island off Texas was the scene of the first successful launch of a space vehicle by an American company.

"Conestoga I," owned by Space Services Incorporated of America, climbed skyward to the cheers of investors shouting, "Long live free enterprise!" Named for the wagons that carried the settlers west, it heralds the beginning of a new era that challenges individual men and women to dream great dreams and dare to fulfill them.